"I MUST ASK YOU NOT TO IMPORTUNE ME AGAIN, LORD WAKEFORD!"

Letty faced Jules, an expression of distress and determination on her face. "Your action may have caught me off guard, to my shame, but I shall never again allow myself to be put in such a position."

"Oh?" Lord Wakeford replied. "Are you going to tell me your feelings have changed? I shall not believe it. Did it ever occur to you that you do not love your fiancé, that, in fact, you love another?"

Letty turned away, but Lord Wakeford grasped hold of her with unexpected strength and pulled her to him. Caught off guard, Letty responded to his insistent kiss . . .

10/92

A Memorable Collection of Regency Romances

BY ANTHEA MALCOLM AND VALERIE KING

THE COUNTERFEIT HEART (3425, $3.95/$4.95)
by Anthea Malcolm

Nicola Crawford was hardly surprised when her cousin's betrothed disappeared on some mysterious quest. Anyone engaged to such an unromantic, but handsome man was bound to run off sooner or later. Nicola could never entrust her heart to such a conventional, but so deucedly handsome man. . . .

THE COURTING OF PHILIPPA (2714, $3.95/$4.95)
by Anthea Malcolm

Miss Philippa was a very successful author of romantic novels. Thus she was chagrined to be snubbed by the handsome writer Henry Ashton whose own books she admired. And when she learned he considered love stories completely beneath his notice, she vowed to teach him a thing or two about the subject of love. . . .

THE WIDOW'S GAMBIT (2357, $3.50/$4.50)
by Anthea Malcolm

The eldest of the orphaned Neville sisters needed a chaperone for a London season. So the ever-resourceful Livia added several years to her age, invented a deceased husband, and became the respectable Widow Royce. She was certain she'd never regret abandoning her girlhood until she met dashing Nicholas Warwick. . . .

A DARING WAGER (2558, $3.95/$4.95)
by Valerie King

Ellie Dearborne's penchant for gaming had finally led her to ruin. It seemed like such a lark, wagering her devious cousin George that she would obtain the snuffboxes of three of society's most dashing peers in one month's time. She could easily succeed, too, were it not for that exasperating Lord Ravenworth. . . .

THE WILLFUL WIDOW (3323, $3.95/$4.95)
by Valerie King

The lovely young widow, Mrs. Henrietta Harte, was not all inclined to pursue the sort of romantic folly the persistent King Brandish had in mind. She had to concentrate on marrying off her penniless sisters and managing her spendthrift mama. Surely Mr. Brandish could fit in with her plans somehow . . .

Available wherever paperbacks are sold, or order direct from the Publisher. Send cover price plus 50¢ per copy for mailing and handling to Zebra Books, Dept. 3810, 475 Park Avenue South, New York, N.Y. 10016. Residents of New York and Tennessee must include sales tax. DO NOT SEND CASH. For a free Zebra/Pinnacle catalog please write to the above address.

First Season
Anne Baldwin

ZEBRA BOOKS
KENSINGTON PUBLISHING CORP.

ZEBRA BOOKS

are published by

Kensington Publishing Corp.
475 Park Avenue South
New York, NY 10016

First printing: July, 1992

Printed in the United States of America

Chapter One

"Please, Papa, may I go to London for the Season this year?" Laetitia Biddle begged. "What is the purpose of having a fortune if I may not spend it?"

Squire Biddle shifted his heavy bulk in the velvet-upholstered chair, turning to look at his wife. Edith Biddle laid her embroidery on the window seat and spread her hands out palms up, indicating that the decision was up to her husband. Their daughter's plea was not a new one. Since she had inherited the considerable fortune of fifty thousand pounds from her paternal aunt two years earlier, Letty's only thoughts had been of a London Season. Such a dream was understandable in a girl of eighteen in this Year of our Lord 1803, but London was far from the Derbyshire countryside in more ways than distance.

Squire Biddle turned back to his daughter, sighing heavily. Letty stood quietly before him, hands clenched behind her slim frame, her blue eyes entreating, waiting eagerly for his answer. For a moment Squire Biddle stared unseeingly at the dark oak-beamed parlor ceiling, trying to avoid those eyes and make a just decision. Finally he spoke.

"I know every young girl must long for a London Season," he said carefully, "but the reality may be very different from your hopes. You must consider, Letty, that you have been raised entirely in country society. You have not once been to London, or even a large town. You may not find the city comfortable. You would also be among strangers. Your mother and I do not have the proper connections to present you in Society. You would have to stay with your aunt, *if* she were willing to sponsor you."

"Aunt Henrietta is Mother's sister, so she must be agreeable," Letty interrupted. "I know London would be very different from Derbyshire. That is why I wish to go."

Letty took a deep breath and quickly marshaled her arguments in favor of a London Season, silently willing her parents to understand.

"I am all of eighteen years, Papa. I shall be too old to be presented if you do not allow me to go this year. If I stay here in Derbyshire, how shall I meet any eligible gentlemen? There is only Tom," she said, referring to the son of a prosperous farmer in the district.

Letty's father and mother exchanged helpless looks. They had no forceful arguments to present in favor of her staying, although they would have preferred to bring Letty out in their quiet society. It *was* true there were few eligible gentlemen in the district, and none of high social status. Lord Woodburn was already married, as was Sir Archer. Was it fair to deny Letty a London Season when she had the money to finance it and her aunt would probably be willing to take on the responsibility of presenting her?

"Very well, Letty," the squire said rather heavily. "You may go if your aunt agrees to sponsor you."

"Oh, thank you, Papa," Letty cried, flinging herself at her father and hugging him tightly, adding to the creases in his collared vest and linen shirt.

"And you, too, Mother," she said, going to her

mother and kissing her cheek. Mrs. Biddle returned the kiss, looking at her excited daughter indulgently. Letty was almost dancing with happiness at the prospect of her dream of a London Season coming true at last.

"You must remember to obey your aunt as you would us," her mother reminded her. "She will stand in our place during your stay there."

"Of course," Letty agreed happily, turning about the room, a faraway look in her eyes. "I must go tell Daisy," she exclaimed suddenly, remembering that the news would be as welcome to her young maid as it had been to her. With a final hug to each of her parents, she ran out of the room.

Squire Biddle arose from his comfortable armchair and joined his wife on the window seat, his usually placid face exhibiting an uncharacteristic gravity.

"I did not see how we could continue to refuse her. It is not an unreasonable request for one of her age and fortune, particularly when your sister resides in London," he said almost defensively.

"No, we could not," Mrs. Biddle agreed. "I only hope the Season may live up to her expectations. My sister Henrietta is not the easiest person to get along with, although she may have changed. I have not seen her for years."

Not since my marriage, Edith Biddle thought to herself, remembering. Her sister had considered a marriage to a simple country squire to be beneath the granddaughter of an earl. Although she had received no other offers in her four-and-twenty years, both her sister and mother would have preferred Edith remain single than marry Squire Biddle. Henrietta had attended the wedding, but she had never made an effort to visit her sister again, nor had she invited Edith to London to visit when she herself had married and moved there eighteen years before.

"I believe Henrietta's daughter Sophie is to make her come-out this year," Mrs. Biddle continued aloud, "so she should be willing to bring out Letty as well. It would not be that much more trouble."

"She will agree if we foot the bill for both girls in order to recompense her for any trouble," Squire Biddle said rather cynically.

"Yes," Mrs. Biddle sighed, her husband's words bringing another problem to mind. "Letty's fortune. *That* is a worry. I'm afraid the combination of Letty's wealth, beauty, and innocence will make her tempting prey to fortune hunters. We shall have to depend upon Henrietta to protect her from them."

They were both silent, wondering anew how they had produced a child like Letty. Squire Biddle was a short, stocky man of florid complexion and rough features, and Mrs. Biddle, while she had an air of definite refinement, was not a handsome woman. Perhaps the Fates, to make up for giving them just the one child, had made her everything they could have asked. Even allowing for their natural prejudice, they knew Letty was an enchanting young girl. She was small and slight, with lustrous dark brown hair, deep blue eyes, and delicate features set in a classically oval face. A generous spirit and captivating manners enhanced her natural beauty.

"I do have control over her fortune until she is of age," the squire said, responding to his wife's earlier comment. "That should keep some of the fortune hunters at bay."

"Yes," Mrs. Biddle agreed. "I shall ask Henrietta to make that fact generally known."

Squire Biddle frowned. He didn't like the idea of the protection of his daughter being in another's hands, even if that other was his wife's sister. Sometimes he almost wished *his* sister had not left her fortune to Letty. Mary Biddle had married a wealthy factory owner in Manchester who had died in an accident only a year later. Mary, having no children of her own, had chosen to leave her entire fortune to her niece. It had been exceedingly generous of her, but having too much money could cause problems. One did not need a great deal of it to be happy, the squire reflected philosophically. He himself had had a very happy life with his hunting and farming, never feeling a desire to go to London to indulge in the amusements found there.

Mrs. Biddle could guess the direction her husband's thoughts were taking by the frown. "Do not worry about Letty," she said reassuringly. "Henrietta will keep her safe if for no other reason than Society would hold her responsible if she did not. For the rest, we must trust to Letty's common sense and upbringing."

"You are right, I know," the squire said with a rueful smile. "I suppose I am hesitant because I shall miss her. This will be the first time she has left us for an extended period of time."

Mrs. Biddle put her hand over his and squeezed it affectionately. "I shall miss her, too, but we must let her go." Feeling tears starting to form in her eyes, she stood up abruptly. "There is no point in delay. I shall write Henrietta directly," she proclaimed, and went to find her letter-case.

Several days later, Henrietta Hardwick sat in the Great Salon of her London town house perusing the morning's post. A frown creased her brow as she finished an especially lengthy communication from her sister.

"What is it, Mama—bad news?" her daughter Sophie asked from her chair nearby, where she was embroidering a fine linen handkerchief.

Lady Hardwick looked up at her daughter and laid the letter on a small round table next to her gilt chair.

"No, it is not precisely bad news. I have a letter from my sister Edith in Derbyshire. She wishes me to present her daughter along with you this spring."

"Oh, no, Mama," Sophie protested, a look of dismay coming over her face. "It is *my* come-out. I do not wish to be presented with a country cousin. Think what it would do to my credit."

"In the ordinary course of events I would not consider such a scheme," her mother agreed, "but there are some extenuating circumstances. Laetitia was left a large fortune by her paternal aunt some two years ago. Regrettably, it is from trade, but it is a considerable fortune nonetheless—fifty thousand pounds. Members of the *ton* who would usually not invite us to their entertainments would do so if Laetitia were to stay with us this Season. Money always opens doors, wherever it is from. In addition, Squire Biddle offers to stand for the entire cost of presenting both of you if I take on the responsibility of his daughter. This would allow us, among other things, to have our gowns done by a better modiste and to engage more servants."

Sophie, whose slightly plump face had been taking on a sulky aspect at the idea of being presented with a provincial cousin with a fortune from trade, brightened at this last.

"Yes, that would be good, Mama," she said slowly, "but what does she look like?" No matter how rich her cousin was, she would refuse to be presented with anyone who cast her into the shade.

"I do not know," Lady Hardwick admitted. "I have

not ever seen her. But neither my sister nor Squire Biddle are even passably handsome, so it's extremely unlikely Laetitia would be either. Squire Biddle is a heavy, coarse-looking man, and my sister is large and horse-faced. Although my mother and I deplored Edith marrying a simple squire, we knew that with her looks, she was unlikely to receive a better offer."

Lady Hardwick lapsed into silence, thinking with satisfaction of her own marriage to a baron. Although it did gall her that her title of Lady, as the widow of a baron, was one only of courtesy and not one to which she was entitled, a baron was a great deal better than a squire. And *her* daughter, she was determined, would marry high enough to have the *right* to the title "Lady."

She looked at her daughter with satisfaction. Sophie had the slightly plump good looks presently in vogue. It was a pity her hair was not of a lighter shade of blond, but washes of camomile tea and careful choices of the colors of her gowns made it appear lighter than it was. No fault could be found with her features, and if her face was a little round, judicious choice of hair styles minimized it.

Sophie had been thinking of the possibilities created by access to more money for the Season. "Could we buy a new carriage, Mama? Our barouche is sadly out of fashion."

"I do not see why not," Lady Hardwick replied, smiling indulgently at her daughter. "One's mode of transportation is noticed by Society and must be in keeping with one's rank, so it would be a legitimate expense to charge to the squire." She saw that her daughter was becoming reconciled to sharing her come-out with her cousin, and pressed her advantage. "Laetitia's presence will hardly be noticed, much less detract from yours. In fact, far from detracting from

11

you, I believe the presence of Laetitia will only add to your credit. How much more pleasing your appearance and manners must appear when compared to an awkward country cousin's. It will only be necessary to see that her behavior is not so outrageous that it embarrasses us. That would do us all harm."

"What about her fortune?" Sophie questioned, a disquieting thought occurring to her. "Will not the eligible gentlemen be more interested in her than in me? I have little more than a competence."

"You must remember that while Laetitia's fortune is large, it comes from trade. Gentlemen who are willing to overlook that fact will most likely be those pressed for money, and they would not be among your court to begin with. It will present a problem in getting her acceptably married off, though," Henrietta mused. "Edith requests that I protect Laetitia from fortune hunters, but they are very likely the only ones who will be interested in her. I suppose I can marry her off to a wealthy cit or an elderly gentleman of the minor nobility who will be attracted by her youth and not be overly concerned about her lack of breeding and looks."

"Perhaps you have the right of it, Mama," Sophie began, and then suddenly exclaimed in distress, "Almack's, Mama! She would never be given vouchers, and if I am not able to attend the assemblies there, I shall never meet the most eligible gentlemen."

Lady Hardwick frowned. Her daughter had a valid point. Laetitia Biddle would never be given a voucher to the exclusive "marriage mart," and if the patronesses knew Miss Biddle would be staying with Lady Hardwick for the Season, they might choose not to approve Sophie either, rather than admit just one of a pair of girls sharing a come-out.

"I believe we may be able to solve that problem,"

she said slowly. "I shall not tell anyone I plan to sponsor Laetitia until you have already received your voucher. That way the patronesses will not be put in the position of having to consider awarding only one voucher to a household with two girls making their come-outs. Then, when your cousin does arrive, I believe Society will understand if you attend and Letty does not. Surely they would not expect you to refuse after you have already been awarded a voucher."

"Very well, Mama," Sophie agreed after thinking over her mother's points. "I suppose it will do no harm to share my come-out with her so long as you do not expect us to become bosom-bows."

"No, indeed." Lady Hardwick smiled, pleased to have won her point. "We shall put her in the small bedchamber on the ground floor, out of our way."

The matter decided, Lady Hardwick went to pen a reply to her sister, leaving Sophie to dream of all the things she would be able to purchase this Season with her cousin's money.

Chapter Two

"Oh, look, Daisy, have you ever seen so many carriages?" Letty asked, looking excitedly out the window of their coach as it clattered slowly through the streets of London.

"No, Miss Letty," replied Daisy, who was looking out the window with as much fascination as her mistress. Neither girl had ever been out of Derbyshire before, and they had spent the entire trip glued to the windows, suffering from none of the boredom that commonly afflicts more seasoned travelers. "It do smell, though, don't it?" Daisy added, wrinkling her freckled nose as the less than salubrious odors of London invaded the carriage.

Letty, however, was not willing to admit that anything could be wrong with London. "I am sure we shall get used to it," she said dismissively. "London! There are so *many* people, just look."

The two girls continued to watch the passing scene with wonder, neither noting the ragged clothes on some of the passersby, nor the despairing faces. They saw only the color and bustle of the great city, so different from the quiet Derbyshire countryside. Street vendors raucously called their wares, post boys in bright coats rang their handbells, sedan chair carriers

14

jostled pedestrians on the sidewalks as they made way for their rich passengers, and carriages finished in lustrous lacquer clattered over the streets.

"Oh, I just *know* the Season will be wonderful," Letty enthused, her blue eyes sparkling with anticipation.

"Yes, miss. Who would have thought we'd go to London for a Season?" Daisy marveled.

After a while the girls noticed the streets were becoming less crowded, and the sidewalks cleaner. The buildings of wood and brick made way for rows of neat gray Portland stone town houses, differing from each other only in the style and color of their front doors.

"These look like fashionable residences. We must be nearing my aunt's," Letty conjectured, straightening her blue merino dress and plain brown traveling cloak. "Do I look presentable, Daisy? I do so wish to make a good impression."

Daisy looked her mistress over critically. The days of travel had left no trace of fatigue on Letty's young face, and her clothes, if a little creased, were clean and neat.

"You look fine, miss," Daisy reassured her, smoothing her own dress. She did not wish to appear too provincial to the fine London servants.

Letty's guess that they were near her aunt's proved to be correct, for the carriage presently rolled to a stop. A groom opened the carriage door, lowering the steps for the passengers, while a postilion knocked at the door of the town house. Letty descended from the carriage carefully, surveying the house with interest. It looked rather small, being only three windows across and three floors high, but then, the others in the street were just as small, she noted. She went slowly up the few steps to the front door, admiring the decorative iron railings and the ornate stucco designs adorning the pilasters.

The door had opened to the postilion's knock, and Letty, followed closely by her maid, stepped into a small but attractive entrance hall.

"This way, if you please, Miss Biddle," a liveried footman said, relieving Letty of her cape and leading her to a small parlor that opened off to the right of the hall.

Letty, feeling a little apprehensive for the first time since she had left home, looked regretfully after Daisy, who was being led away into the interior of the house by another footman. Resolutely banishing the feeling, Letty stepped past the footman into the room.

"If you will wait here, I shall inform Lady Hardwick that you have arrived," the footman said, shutting the door behind him as he left.

Letty looked around the small salon with interest. She had never seen anything like it. The walls had been painted with various Greek designs: urns, swags of honeysuckle, palm trees, and numerous gods and goddesses. A finely woven carpet with a central floral motif surrounded by a border in the Greek key design covered the floor, and four elaborate Corinthian columns stood in the center of the room. Letty had a sensation of having stepped back in time into a Greek temple. Her aunt must have decorated in the latest mode, she thought appreciatively. Letty was accustomed to houses with ceilings of dark-aged oak beams and walls covered with heavy tapestries, and the light, airy feeling of this room was a pleasant novelty. She took a turn about the room, admiring the furnishings, and then sat down on a delicate japanned and gilded chair to wait for her aunt.

A few minutes later she heard steps approaching

and stood, eager to greet her aunt. The footman opened the door and a handsome woman of middle age entered, followed by a girl who looked to be near Letty's own age. Letty would have gone forward to embrace them, but something about their demeanor restrained her. She stood silently, waiting for her aunt to speak first, and taking in their appearance. Her aunt was a handsome woman, if a bit heavy and with improbably light blond hair. Her cousin was also slightly plump, and had darker blond hair and pale blue eyes. Both mother and daughter were clad in fashionable gowns of thin muslin, the sight of which drew an inaudible sigh of envy from Letty.

A look of dismay crossed the faces of Lady Hardwick and her daughter as they surveyed Letty. This was not the horse-faced provincial they had expected. Even in her outmoded blue merino gown the beauty of Letty's face and form was undeniable.

Letty saw the look of dismay but misinterpreted it. She looked down at her gown deprecatingly. "I know I must look a fright after the journey. Please forgive my appearance."

Lady Hardwick recovered from her shock at the sight of her niece. "Of course. One never looks one's best after days of travel. You need not apologize," she said graciously as she stepped forward. "I am your aunt Henrietta, and this is your cousin Sophie. We are pleased to welcome you to London."

Letty curtsied, and then her spontaneous heart moved her to embrace her aunt warmly.

"Thank you for agreeing to sponsor me this season, Aunt Henrietta," she said, and then turned to her cousin. "And thank you for agreeing to share your come-out with me. I have so looked forward to having a cousin my age with whom to be friends," she said, hugging her as well.

Sophie returned the embrace halfheartedly, causing Letty a moment of hurt which she quickly routed by reminding herself that she could not expect them to be friends right off. It would take time to get to know each other. Perhaps her cousin was a little shy.

Lady Henrietta observed Letty's actions with some relief. At least the girl appeared biddable. Perhaps all was not lost. Then she noted Sophie's unenthusiastic response and the sullen look that appeared on her face. She would have some trouble with her daughter, she could see. Sophie had realized that she would be outshone by her cousin. Lady Henrietta decided she had best deal with the situation immediately.

"I am sure you will wish to freshen up from your journey," she said to her niece, picking up a bell on a small table and ringing it briskly. "Show Miss Biddle to her bedchamber," she instructed the footman who responded.

She turned back to her niece. "I shall have your supper sent to you on a tray tonight, as I am sure you will wish to retire early after the fatigues of such a long journey. We shall become better acquainted in the morning."

With more words of thanks Letty took her leave of her aunt and cousin and followed the footman from the room.

Sophie closed the door to the salon as soon as the footman and Letty had left and turned to face her mother accusingly.

"You told me she was horse-faced."

"I said her mother is," Lady Hardwick said, correcting herself. She sat in the chair Letty had vacated and motioned her daughter to sit as well. "How Edith and her uncouth husband managed to produce a daughter like Laetitia, I cannot imagine," she muttered.

"Could we not send her back?" Sophie pleaded, rising and pacing the floor in her agitation.

"Don't be nonsensical," Lady Hardwick said firmly, although she did not like the situation any better than did her daughter. It was *most* unfortunate that Laetitia had turned out to be a beauty. "We have already spent a great deal of the money her father sent, and I have told many of my friends I am sponsoring my niece. I do not wish it to appear that I am not doing my duty. And you are forgetting her money will open doors to us this Season that would otherwise remain closed."

Sophie recognized the truth of her mother's words, but she was still far from reconciled to the situation. "We *cannot* be presented together," she wailed. "She will far outshine me."

"Not necessarily," Lady Hardwick said slowly. "There are ways we may prevent her from appearing to her full advantage. Do not forget, *I* am in charge of her wardrobe. I shall order only the most unbecoming styles and colors. All is not lost."

Sophie sat back down and gradually allowed herself to be somewhat pacified, but at that moment she conceived an intense hatred of the cousin she had been willing to patronize and condescend to before she had seen her beauty.

Letty followed the footman to a small bedchamber on the ground floor, where she found Daisy busily unpacking her trunks. Letty looked around the room with pleasure. Lady Hardwick had assigned her niece to the smallest and most unfashionably decorated bedchamber, but Letty did not know this, and thought the room charming. There was a small bed with gracefully carved posters, several square-backed

19

Chippendale chairs, a matching mahogany writing desk, a washing stand, and a breakfast table with a latticed compartment for food. A flowered carpet in soft pinks and greens felt deliciously soft beneath her feet. The faint feeling of unease that had come with the restrained welcome she had received from her aunt and cousin retreated, and her excitement at being in London returned.

"Is it not beautiful, Daisy?" she asked, looking appreciatively about the room. "Aunt Henrietta has such a modishly decorated house. She and cousin Sophie were dressed in the latest fashions, too," she added. "It will be wonderful to have a London wardrobe. I just know I am going to enjoy this Season above all things."

"I hope so, miss," Daisy replied as she continued unpacking. She was not so optimistic for herself. The servants here appeared to be quite top-lofty, and had so far treated her with an unconcealed disdain for her country origins.

Letty awoke early the next morning to a medley of unfamiliar sounds. For a moment she did not know where she was, and felt uncomfortably disoriented. Then full consciousness returned and she remembered. A feeling of joy coursed through her. She was in London! She slipped from her bed and went to the window to see what was occasioning the racket outside, but was disappointed to find the window overlooked only a bare yard and carriage house. The only sign of life was a servant girl crossing the yard to begin her duties. Letty remained at the window nevertheless, dreaming of the Season before her, not even noticing when Daisy left to get some hot water for her mistress.

Daisy returned with the water and Letty left the window to wash and prepare for the day. Daisy was brushing Letty's lustrous dark hair when a knock sounded at the door and a maid entered the room with a breakfast tray. After a quick curtsy to Letty, she placed the tray on the breakfast table and left. Daisy patted a final curl into place and Letty went to see what was served for breakfast in London. The tray held a pot of chocolate and paper-thin slices of bread with butter. Letty looked at the bread wonderingly.

"Look how *white* the bread is, Daisy," she said, breaking a piece off and holding it out for her maid to sample. "Even the bread is finer in London," she said, biting into a piece. A surprised look came over her face as the flavor registered.

"How odd it tastes, does it not?" she asked, slathering the remaining piece with butter to mask the taste.

Daisy bit into hers cautiously. "So it does. Wonder what's in it?"

"I do not know. I suppose we are just accustomed to country foods," Letty replied, unaware that London bakers added chalk, alum, and bone ashes to their bread to make it whiter.

She finished the bread and drank her chocolate gratefully. The chocolate, at least, was no different from what she was used to. By the time she finished her drink, the hour was nearing ten o'clock. She decided her aunt and cousin must be up, and with a final look in the glass to be sure she appeared her best, went to find them.

She did not see her relatives in the salon she had been received in the prior afternoon. Spying a footman in the hall outside, she asked him to direct her to them.

"I believe they are in the Grand Salon, Miss Biddle," he informed her, and on her expressing her ignorance as to its location, offered to show her where it was. He led her up a staircase with a wrought-iron balustrade located behind the entrance hall to a large salon at the front of the first floor. It was an imposing room, decorated attractively in the neoclassical style with Greek columns, busts of gods and goddesses, and symmetrical stucco designs. The walls were not painted as they had been in the salon below, but were covered with ivory damasked silk. There were several comfortable-looking armchairs and sofas arranged around two carved marble fireplaces, and gilt side chairs against the walls. Her aunt was sitting in an armchair near one of the fireplaces.

"Good morning, Aunt Henrietta," Letty said as she entered the room.

"Good morning, Laetitia," her aunt responded. "I trust you are recovered from the fatigues of your journey?"

When Letty assured her she was, her aunt motioned her to a gilt chair upholstered in sleek ivory satin damask.

"We have a great deal to do to make you presentable for the Season," her aunt said in a businesslike manner. "We shall go shopping this morning and order you a new wardrobe so it will be done before the entertainments of the Season begin. Then," she said in a tone of voice that indicated Letty was in for a rare treat, "we have been invited to attend dinner at the home of the Duchess of Grimwold. It is not entirely correct for you and Sophie to attend, since you have not yet had your come-out ball, but one does not refuse a duchess. She wishes to be the first to present the new heiress."

Lady Hardwick's announcement had all the effect on her niece she could have wished. Letty's eyes sparkled with anticipation. She, Letty Biddle, a simple squire's daughter, was to dine with a duchess! Her aunt's reference to her niece as an heiress passed over Letty's head.

"Will there be time to shop for a new wardrobe and be ready for dinner by one?" Letty worried.

Her aunt looked at her in surprise. "Dinner at one o'clock? Only the servants have dinner at midday. This is *London*, Laetitia. We normally dine at eight. Supper is at eleven. If one desires to have something between breakfast and dinner, one may have a small nuncheon."

At Letty's look of surprise, her aunt decided it was time to give her niece a short lecture. "I realize you are used to country ways, Laetitia, but you must endeavor to disguise this as much as possible. Nothing will sink you so quickly in the eyes of Society as to appear provincial. It would also reflect on your cousin and myself. I hope you will endeavor to behave at all times so as to be a credit to us."

Letty felt abashed. She would not wish to cause the credit of her relatives to go down as a result of their kindness in presenting her to Society.

"I shall do my best, Aunt Henrietta," she assured her aunt. "I realize that I do not know all the ways of Society here in London, but I shall try hard to learn."

Her aunt looked satisfied and stood, saying briskly, "Now, if you are ready, I shall summon Sophie and we shall go to the modiste's."

The new carriage, bought with the squire's money, delivered them shortly to Madame Parenteau's, Pall Mall. Refugees from the troubles in France had been arriving in London for several years, and the English ladies of the *haut ton* had been quick to discover that many of these displaced Frenchwomen made superior modistes. Madame Parenteau was one of the most exclusive.

They were attended by Madame Parenteau herself, who had already heard of the young heiress and that her aunt was sponsoring her. She showed them into a private room and gave them pattern books to look through while assistants brought in materials for their inspection. Letty and Sophie eagerly turned the pages of the pattern books together, Sophie momentarily forgetting her hatred of her cousin in the realization that it was due to Letty's money that they were able to patronize this best of modistes.

"Look, Mama, may I have a gown like this?" Sophie asked, pointing to a drawing of a short, full frock worn over an elaborately trimmed underdress.

"That is the tunic dress, Lady Hardwick," Madame Parenteau explained. "It is the rage in Paris, and is just being introduced here in London."

Lady Hardwick looked at the drawing critically. It would be good for Sophie to appear at the forefront of fashion, but the layered fullness would emphasize Sophie's plumpness.

"I think not," she decided. "This would be more appropriate," she said, pointing to a drawing of a simple gown in the Grecian mode. The clean lines and soft folds would minimize Sophie's curves. "In the pale blue muslin and peach sarcenet."

Lady Hardwick continued to select patterns and materials for her daughter's and her own wardrobes rapidly and with an unerring eye for the styles and colors that were most flattering. Then she turned her attention to her niece.

"Perhaps the tunic dress for Miss Biddle," Madame Parenteau suggested, knowing it would look charming on one of Letty's slight figure.

24

"No," Lady Hardwick said, looking at her niece assessingly. "This one, I think," she said, pointing to a drawing of a frock with a fitted bodice.

The Frenchwoman looked at the pattern dubiously, uncertain whether to offer her opinion that it would not be flattering to the girl.

"In the fawn-colored muslin and sage-green silk," Lady Hardwick instructed.

At this choice of colors, Madame Parenteau, who was an astute woman, realized that Lady Hardwick was intentionally ordering unflattering gowns for the girl. Looking at the two girls sitting together, she understood. It was natural a mother would not desire her daughter to be outshone by another. It was a pity, though, for Miss Biddle would have been a joy to dress attractively. Lady Hardwick was paying the bills, however, so Madame Parenteau gave a Gallic shrug and aligned herself with the older woman.

"Of course, Lady Hardwick, excellent choices," she said, making the notation on her list.

Lady Hardwick went on to select the rest of Letty's wardrobe without any input from her niece. Letty was disappointed, for she had hoped to choose her own gowns, but she reminded herself how stylish her aunt and cousin always looked, and made no protest.

Next the trio went to the milliner's and haberdasher's for hats, gloves, shoes, parasols, fans, and other accessories. Letty was overwhelmed by the variety of goods available, and would have liked to look for hours, but Lady Hardwick wished to return home with plenty of time to prepare for the dinner at the Duchess of Grimwold's.

Once they arrived home, Lady Hardwick instructed Sophie to lend Letty one of her gowns to wear at the dinner, as she was sure nothing Letty had brought from Derbyshire would be suitable. Letty dressed for the dinner with a feeling of great anticipation. The gown Sophie had lent her was a pink chemise-robe that fastened from neck to hem with tiny shell buttons. It was large for Letty's slight figure, but Daisy skillfully pinned it to fit. As Daisy brushed and arranged Letty's hair in front of the glass, Letty felt she hardly knew herself, she looked so fine. What an experience it would be to write home about, dining with a duchess!

With a final look in the glass, Letty went to join her aunt and cousin in the Grand Salon. Lady Hardwick was clad in a gown of cream and gold striped silk, and Sophie was in a white muslin gown edged in trim of a classical motif. How fine *they* looked, Letty thought, and was less happy with her own appearance. Soon, when she got her new gowns, she would look equally fine, she consoled herself.

Her aunt scrutinized Letty carefully and nodded her approval. "You do know how to behave yourself, I hope, Laetitia? You have attended dinners in the country?" she questioned.

"Yes, of course, Aunt," Letty reassured her.

A footman told them the carriage was ready, and they went down to the street.

They traveled very slowly through the crowded streets, for all the fashionable world was beginning to bestir itself at eight and set out for the first of the evening's entertainments. Letty wanted to ask her cousin Sophie about the duchess, but Sophie pointedly kept her head turned away from Letty, and they rode in silence. Finally the carriage stopped, and Letty prepared to get out.

"Not yet, Laetitia," her aunt said impatiently. "We do not alight from the carriage until it stops before the door. It will be a few minutes yet, as there are many carriages and we must wait our turn."

The few minutes turned out to be closer to a half hour, and Letty was beside herself with excitement by the time the carriage stopped for the last time. The carriage doors were opened by footmen in elaborate livery holding flambeaux. They let down the carriage steps and handed out the passengers. Letty descended in a daze, looking at the brightly lit house before her in awe. It was not a town house like her aunt's, but a large detached house of a size to equal the great houses in the country. A carpet led from the carriage up the stairs and into the house, and curious bystanders lined its edges, gawking at the gentry in their fine clothes.

Letty followed her aunt and cousin up the steps and into the house, where the duchess stood to receive her guests. Still in a daze, Letty was presented to the Duchess of Grimwold, and just had the presence of mind to sink into a curtsy with a muffled "Your Grace."

"So this is the heiress," the duchess boomed in a loud voice. "Pretty, but no countenance," she proclaimed, turning from her dismissively and speaking to her next guest.

Letty passed on down the line, not even registering the duchess's rudeness, being too concerned trying to remember the names and faces of the people to whom she was being presented. They passed into a huge salon lit with glittering chandeliers. The room was magnificent. It was decorated in the ornate French rococo style popular in the 1770s. The white walls and ceilings were lavishly covered with gilt stucco designs of intertwined wreaths and festoons, and an ornately carved fireplace of veined marble dominated one end of the room. Everywhere candles glittered in elaborate chandeliers, their light reflected in the magnificent jewels worn by the guests. Letty was looking open-mouthed at a huge looking-glass framed in an elaborately carved and gilded wood, when she felt an elbow jab her sharply in her ribs.

"Don't gawk so," her cousin hissed at her. Letty supposed her cousin had a point and tried to keep her eyes downcast, staying close to her aunt's skirts so that she would not lose her in the press of people. She had no conception of the time passing, but was becoming very tired, and when she realized they had come into the dining room, she hoped they would be able to rest. Letty had hoped to sit near her aunt and cousin, but found herself separated from them and seated between two unknown gentlemen. Or, rather, one unknown gentleman, she corrected herself, for she thought she remembered having been presented to the older gentleman at her left, although she could not remember his name. She glanced about the room, which was as elaborately decorated with gilt stucco as the others, and found herself looking into the green eyes of the gentleman seated across from her. He was *very* handsome, she thought appreciatively, noting his wavy chestnut hair, tightly fitting coat, and immaculate linen. Then, remembering her cousin's admonition not to gawk, she looked down at her place, but not before she registered an amused smile on the lips of the handsome gentleman.

The other guests began their soup, and Letty followed suit. It was delicious, a creamy brown soup with a flavor of Madeira.

After the soup, the servants began removing the covers of the many dishes on the table, releasing a bouquet of delicious odors. While they were thus employed, Letty dared to glance around the table, remarking the fine raiment of the guests. The gentlemen wore tight-fitting coats and sparkling white linen, and the women were clad in gold- and silver-embroidered muslins of incredible fineness, adorned with magnificent jewels. For the first time, some of Letty's excitement left, and she began to feel nervous. What did she know of dining with duchesses? She began to fear she might inadvertently do something wrong. A voice interrupted her thoughts, and she turned to the gentleman on her left, who was addressing polite comments to her. Letty, embarrassed by not being able to remember his name or rank, felt her face redden, and answered in monosyllables. He turned his attention to the woman on his left, and Letty looked at the dishes placed before her.

There were two dishes on the table before Letty, what appeared to be stewed fish, and a dish of neat's tongue. Seeing that the other guests were helping themselves to the dishes before them, Letty followed suit. The gentleman on her left offered her some of the dish that had been before him, and Letty accepted. Then, lest her manners be found lacking, she picked up the dish of neat's tongue to offer it to the gentleman on her right. But that exquisite gentleman was deep in conversation with the lady on his right, and did not notice her action. Letty hesitated, unsure what to do. Should she offer it to the gentleman on her left, or did one offer only dishes to the person at one's right? Or was it possible it was only gentlemen who offered dishes to ladies? She realized the informal dinner parties she had attended in Derbyshire had not prepared her for this. She returned the neat's tongue to its original place before her and looked at the other diners, trying to see what they did. It was then that she noticed the many liveried servants standing around the side of the room. Occasionally one would leave his place and offer a dish to a guest. With some relief, she decided it was their duty to offer guests dishes, and began to eat again. However, no servants came to offer *her* any dishes, and Letty found herself confined to eating the dishes originally before her, supplemented by two more the gentleman on her left offered. She finished the stewed fish, and served herself more neat's tongue. She did not particularly care for neat's tongue, not liking its firm texture, but she felt she must eat something lest she make herself conspicuous by just sitting.

Suddenly the loud voice of the duchess was heard over the low buzz of conversation.

"Brampton, where is the neat's tongue? You know I am particularly fond of neat's tongue."

There was a quick whispered exchange among the servants, and one went to pick up the dish before Letty, on which only one serving remained.

The duchess noticed the one serving on the plate.

"What d'ye mean, gel, keeping all the neat's tongue for yourself?" she demanded. "Strange behavior for a guest, but then, an heiress may do as she pleases, I suppose. Much like a duchess, heh, gel?" she concluded, laughing loudly.

Letty felt herself blush in mortification as the regard of the whole table was momentarily focused on her. She did not dare look anywhere but straight ahead, and even that was not safe, for she found herself looking into the amused green eyes of the chestnut-haired gentleman. She dropped her gaze to her plate, and fortunately the duchess turned the attention of the guests back to the servants.

"Well, why are you all standing about like loobies? Get me some more," she commanded, and, dismissing the incident, engaged one of her neighbors in conversation.

Letty felt some of the color retreat from her face as the guests went back to their meals, but she still felt excruciatingly uncomfortable. She was afraid to look anywhere, and kept her eyes determinedly on her plate. Finally the dishes of the first course were removed, and those of the second course placed on the table. Letty attempted to eat, but the food stuck in her throat. It seemed to be hours before the dinner was over. At last coffee was served and the women left the table to the men and their port. Letty found her aunt and cousin and stayed close to them, feeling safe in their company, although she sensed they were angry with her. Because of the neat's tongue, no doubt, she sighed inwardly. Her suspicions were borne out as soon as they entered the carriage to go home, and Sophie turned to her mother with a martyred look.

"Mama, I was never so embarrassed in my life."

Lady Hardwick looked at Letty with an expression, visible even in the dim light of the carriage, that told Letty she seconded her daughter's feelings.

"Laetitia, I thought you told me you had attended formal dinners. What did you mean by consuming all of one dish yourself?"

Letty looked miserably at the floor of the carriage. "There were only two dishes in front of me. The gentleman on my left offered me some of the one before him, but the first course lasted so *long*. I had to eat something. I did not want to sit doing nothing."

"Why did you not ask your neighbors to pass some of the dishes before them?" Lady Hardwick asked in exasperation. "How do you conduct yourself at dinners in the country?"

"At home we take some of the dish before us and then pass it to our neighbors."

"Then why did you not do the same here?" demanded her aunt.

"I am not sure." Letty tried to explain. "I thought maybe things were done differently here. And then I saw all the servants . . ." She faltered and stopped.

"The servants are there to put the dishes of the various courses on the table and remove those of the last. Much as they do in the country, I am sure," Lady Hardwick finished with some asperity.

Letty raised her head to look at her aunt, pleading for understanding. "But I saw them give dishes to a woman across the table."

"If you wish a servant to get a dish for you, you must ask. What did you imagine? There are over a hundred dishes on the table at such a dinner. If the servants were to offer each guest some of every dish on the table, no one would have time to eat."

Letty made no reply. She felt very stupid. Why had she not done as her instincts had told her? Why had she frozen?

"I can see I made a mistake to imagine that my sister raised you with even the most rudimentary knowledge of how to get along in polite Society," Lady Hardwick continued. "I shall have to catechize you and discover just what you know and do not know before we go anywhere else. Fortunately for you, this evening the duchess was disposed to find your faux pas amusing. The next hostess may not," she finished.

"I am sorry, Aunt Henrietta," Letty said, knowing her apology was inadequate but not knowing what else she could say. She glanced at her cousin, hoping to find some sympathy there, but the look on Sophie's face could be described only as gloating.

Once back at the town house, Letty went directly to her room after bidding her relatives good night. Daisy had fallen asleep in an armchair, waiting for her return. Letty did not wake her, unwilling to hear the excited questions she knew would be forthcoming if she did. She undressed herself and got between the cold sheets of her bed, feeling a complete failure. Tears filled her eyes and she sobbed quietly into her pillow.

Her Season in London was not beginning the way she had imagined. Her aunt was nothing like her mother, and her cousin had not shown a desire to be close to her or even be friendly. Yet she could not blame them for being upset with her; no doubt it had been very embarrassing to them, too. She would try harder. Still, she thought, they could have been a little more understanding.

Chapter Three

Letty woke early again the next morning, aware of a dull pain behind her eyes. She wondered at it a moment, and then remembered the happenings and tears of the night before. She turned over and buried her head in the pillow, but sleep and its merciful oblivion refused to return. She slipped from the bed and padded over the velvety carpet to the window. The view of the carriage house and bare yard disappointed her anew, and she felt a sudden longing for the open spaces of the country.

She glanced at the plain-cased bracket clock above the escritoire. Seven. The servants would just be rising, and her aunt and cousin would probably not be up for hours. Why not go for a walk? Perhaps she could find her way to Hyde Park. Sophie had spoken of it as a place the *haut ton* went to walk and ride. Her spirits lifted at the thought of getting some fresh air. Perhaps a brisk walk would dissipate her headache.

Daisy was not yet awake, so Letty dressed herself in a walking dress and shoes. After a moment's consideration she decided to wear her hooded red wool cape, since the early morning air would be chill.

In the passageway outside her room Letty spotted

a maid carrying a pitcher of hot water and stopped her to ask the way to Hyde Park. The girl looked at Letty with an odd expression, but gave Letty the required directions. Letty let herself out the front door and walked briskly down the street. She found Orchard Street easily, passed Portman Square, continued to Oxford Street, and turned right to Hyde Park as the girl had told her. The sight of the grass and trees revived Letty's spirits. She walked slowly along a path in the park, feeling at home among the greenery. Even the air seemed fresher here, she thought. The park was almost deserted at the early hour; only a few horsemen appeared to be taking advantage of the near-empty lanes to have a gallop.

After she had walked awhile, Letty decided to rest a moment under a tree and review the happenings of the previous night. Her blunder at the duchess's did not seem quite so terrible now, only foolish. She had been a gudgeon to be so overwhelmed by the grandeur of the duchess's residence that she did not use her common sense and do as the other guests. No wonder her aunt Henrietta had been so perturbed with her. She must remember she was ignorant of city ways and try very hard to observe and learn.

This resolution made, Letty felt better and became more aware of her surroundings. She noticed that she seemed to be attracting the attention of the gentlemen going past on horseback. Two men slowed and looked at her quite boldly. A third gentleman, riding a beautiful gray, seemed familiar to Letty. He resembled the wavy-haired gentleman who had sat across from her at the duchess's the night before, Letty thought. He looked at her intently, and Letty returned the gaze. Yes, it was he. He had the same amused smile on his lips that echoed in his eyes. For a moment he looked as though he might speak to her, but then he gave her a mock bow and rode on.

Relieved that he had not spoken to her, Letty decided to go back to her aunt's house lest the rider change his mind and return. She walked quickly back to Adam Street and let herself into the house, hoping to slip back into her room without being noticed. Alas for her plans, as she was crossing the hall her cousin appeared in the doorway of the small salon.

"So there you are, Laetitia. Mama requires you immediately in the Grand Salon. You are in trouble," she finished, a smug look on her plump face. Sophie had chosen to give the message herself instead of having a servant deliver it, preferring that she have the pleasure of informing her cousin of Lady Hardwick's displeasure.

Letty supposed her aunt wished to speak to her again about the night before. Remembering her resolution to try to do as her aunt wished, she did not even stop to take off her cape, but went directly upstairs to the Grand Salon.

"Sophie said you wished to speak to me, Aunt Henrietta?" Letty inquired as she entered the room.

Lady Hardwick, who was seated in one of the satin damask armchairs near the fireplace, turned at her niece's voice and frowned forbiddingly.

"What do you mean, miss, taking a walk by yourself? I could not believe my ears when the maid told me where you had gone.

"And in that cape of all garments," she added, looking at Letty's red wool cape in undisguised horror. "A countrywoman's garment. Although perhaps it was fortunate you wore it, at that. You look like a servant girl in it. Perhaps no one recognized you. Take it off immediately. And I do not wish to see you in it again while you are here."

"But, Aunt, everyone in Derbyshire wears red wool capes. Even Lord Woodburn's wife," Letty protested in bewilderment as she removed the offending garment.

"Please remember that you are no longer in the country, Laetitia," Lady Henrietta said sternly. "Country ways do not do here. Never again are you to wear that cape, and *never* does a lady walk alone *anywhere*. Is that understood? You must always be accompanied by a maid or footman, even if you are going only next door."

"Yes, Aunt," Letty said, thinking it was going to be more difficult to learn the rules of proper behavior in London than she had thought. "I am sorry, Aunt Henrietta, truly I am. I did not realize . . ."

Her aunt seemed to relent a little at Letty's obvious contrition, and motioned her to sit down.

"Well, I suppose one must make allowances for one not given the benefit of being raised in town," Lady Hardwick granted. "But I must say, when Edith asked me to present you, I never realized what a task it would be. Well, it is my duty, and I shall do the best I can. It is fortunate you are an heiress, for Society will be willing to overlook much in one with your wealth. But for the sake of Sophie and myself, I hope you make an effort to behave in a proper manner."

Lady Hardwick then transferred her attention to her daughter, who had followed Letty into the salon to witness her beautiful cousin receiving a dressing down.

"You, Sophie, must help your cousin. I expect you to instruct Laetitia on the behavior proper to one her age and station in Society."

"But, Mama, why must it be my responsibility? She is so ignorant, it will take all my time," Sophie protested ungenerously. She was still not reconciled to sharing her come-out with someone who was not only wealthier, but more beautiful than she. It suited her quite well to have her cousin make a fool of herself.

"Do not forget that Laetitia is under our sponsorship and that her behavior reflects on us. You will do as I say."

"Yes, Mama," Sophie said sullenly with a baleful look at her cousin.

Letty flushed and felt uncomfortable in the face of such obvious dislike. Her dream of having a girl her own age to be friends with was rapidly disappearing.

"You will begin by instructing your cousin in the behavior expected of her at your come-out ball. I plan to hold it next week. You do know how to dance, I trust?" Lady Hardwick asked with a questioning look at her niece.

"Yes, Aunt," Letty replied briefly.

"I am thankful for that, at least. Sophie, I leave you to instruct your cousin, and later I shall expect you both to assist me in making out the invitations for your ball."

Her stern ultimatum delivered, Lady Hardwick stood up and swept regally out of the room, leaving the girls in each other's reluctant company.

Jules Wakeford, Marquess of Thornhill, completed his ride around Hyde Park and then turned his gray toward home. A smile touched his lips as he thought of the young girl in the red cape sitting beneath the tree. She had made a pretty picture with her dark curls peeping beneath the bright red hood, framing her delicate features. She had looked remarkably like the girl who had sat across from him at the dinner the previous night who had eaten all the neat's tongue. Although what a gently-bred girl could be doing out alone in Hyde Park dressed in a servant's cape, he could not imagine.

He was still smiling when he arrived home and went into the breakfast parlor to get another cup of coffee. His younger sister Emily was at the table eating her breakfast. She looked up at his entrance and bade him good morning.

"What is so amusing?" she added, her brother's smile bringing a corresponding one to her face.

Jules looked at his pretty sister affectionately. Although six years separated them, they looked much alike with their fair skin, clear green eyes, and thick chestnut-colored hair. He wondered again why his sister had not married in the three years she had been out. He knew for certain of five offers she had received, and suspected she had stopped twice that many from coming to the point. If she did not quit being so picky, she would end up a spinster, he reflected, for she was already twenty years of age.

"I was just thinking that this Season may prove to be an amusing one after all, with the presence of the Biddle heiress," Jules answered his sister's question.

"The Biddle heiress? I believe I have heard some talk of her. Is she the one being sponsored by Lady Hardwick? I have heard her fortune is considerable."

"Yes, and she is going to need it," Jules said as he sat down at the table with a cup of coffee. He then proceeded to relate to his sister the episode of the neat's tongue at the Duchess of Grimwold's dinner.

"The poor girl," Emily said as Jules finished. "How embarrassed she must have felt!" But even she couldn't restrain a smile at her brother's entertaining manner of telling the story.

"It is obvious she has not the least idea how to go on," Jules said. "I think I saw her in the park this morning, alone and in a servant's cape."

"It is strange Lady Hardwick is not keeping a closer eye on her," Emily mused.

"It will be most diverting to see how Society reacts to Miss Biddle," Jules continued. "Disgust at her manners will war with admiration of her money."

"You make me quite curious to meet her," Emily said. "I shall have to tell Mama to watch for invitations to her presentation ball. I assume we shall receive them, for Mama is acquainted with Lady Hardwick."

"Inform me if we do," Jules said. "I shall attend as well. I cannot afford to miss some good amusement, and I'm sure Miss Biddle will provide it."

"I think you are being wicked, dear brother," Emily remonstrated, "to hope the poor girl makes more mistakes."

Jules merely smiled, and Emily turned the conversation to other subjects, and when he finished his coffee Jules went to dress for his daily appearance at White's. No doubt the Beau would find his anecdotes about the Biddle heiress quite amusing.

* * *

Letty's excitement at being in London gradually returned over the next few days as the memory of her disgrace at the duchess's receded and the day of her come-out ball approached. Lady Hardwick did not allow Letty and Sophie to attend any more entertainments before their formal presentation to Society, but Sophie took her to the circulating library, and Letty went on several short morning calls with her aunt.

Sophie grudgingly instructed Letty in the behavior proper in London Society, and Letty found herself repeating the instructions to herself much of the time. She was determined to make a good impression on Society, and not bring any more disgrace on her aunt. It was going to be very difficult, she feared. There seemed to be so *many* rules in London. Do not dance with someone unless he has been presented to one as a suitable partner by someone one knows; do not meet one's partner's eyes too long; do not go anywhere unattended; do not, do not. Her concentration on the rules caused the ladies Letty met during the morning calls to label her, as had the duchess, "pretty, but no countenance."

One bright spot was the arrival of her new wardrobe from the modiste. She and Daisy unwrapped the parcels eagerly, exclaiming over the fine materials and modish styles. Daisy urged her to try some of them on so that she could see, and Letty willingly complied. Yet, as she viewed herself in the glass, she was aware of a sense of disappointment. Although the gowns were undeniably modish, Letty felt she did not look any better in them than she did in the ones she had brought from Derbyshire. Well, she told herself, she must trust her aunt. Lady

Hardwick undoubtably had excellent taste, for she and Sophie were always in excellent looks.

Letty wrote a letter to her mother and father, telling them of her new wardrobe and the sights of London. However, she did not say much about her aunt and cousin, and as she folded the finished letter, she felt she was not being entirely candid with her parents. It was a new feeling, and not one she liked. Yet she could not tell them of Sophie's puzzling hostility and Lady Hardwick's harshness. Perhaps things would change for the better and she would be able to write of them in the next letter, she thought hopefully as she tied her letter-case shut.

At last the day of the come-out ball arrived. Lady Hardwick had spent the squire's money lavishly in decorating for the ball. Great urns of flowers stood everywhere, and potted palms were placed along the sides of the staircase, creating an exotic walkway to the first floor, where the Grand Salon was to serve as the ballroom. The carpet in the salon had been removed, the floor beeswaxed, and gilt chairs placed along the walls for the chaperones and guests who were not dancing. Supper was to be served in the dining room, and an extra bedchamber and dressing room on the first floor would function as a card room and withdrawing room.

Lady Hardwick had chosen to clothe her daughter and niece in matching gowns of the requisite white muslin for their shared come-out. The pattern she had selected was for a V-necked frock with short sleeves and rather full skirt, trimmed in light blue ribands, and worn with matching light blue silk gloves and slippers. As Daisy helped her mistress into the gown, Letty felt a sense of rising excitement. Daisy brushed her hair until it shone and arranged the curls in as close an approximation of the style *à la* Sappho as she could achieve. Letty selected her garnets from her pitifully meager jewelcase, and after Daisy fastened them about her neck, went to look at herself in the glass. However, the image that confronted her was somehow disappointing. The frock was not very flattering to her, for the deep V-neck emphasized the smallness of her figure, and combined with the full skirt, made her look rather pear-shaped. She hid her disappointment as she thanked Daisy, for the girl had done her best to make her look well, and then went upstairs to find her aunt.

Lady Hardwick and Sophie were already dressed and waiting for Letty in the ballroom. Sophie was looking particularly fine. The gown flattered her fuller figure, and the blue of the trim and accessories was exactly the color of her eyes. Sapphires sparkled at her throat, and the anticipation of the evening had added a glow to the girl that was not usually present.

"How beautiful you look, Cousin Sophie," Letty exclaimed involuntarily as she entered the room.

Letty's compliment was rewarded by the first genuine smile she had received from her cousin. "Thank you," Sophie replied, knowing that she was indeed in her best looks. "You look very fine also," she added condescendingly, thinking privately that her mother had been inspired in her decision to dress them in a style that flattered Sophie much more than it did her cousin. Although Letty's beauty could not be extinguished, it had certainly been dimmed.

Letty and Sophie took their places with Lady Hardwick just inside the door of the ballroom as the guests began to arrive. Letty found herself subjected to sharp scrutiny from the guests, especially the matrons with unmarried daughters in tow.

Letty tried at first to remember all the names, but she was soon overwhelmed by the number of guests. Yet she felt she was acquitting herself creditably, and some of her natural sparkle returned until the Duchess of Grimwold arrived. By virtue of her rank, the duchess went straight to the front of the receiving line. Lady Hardwick welcomed her and Letty curtsied deeply, keeping her eyes on the floor and hoping the duchess would not condescend to remember her, a hope quickly dashed.

"Well, gel," the duchess boomed, "I hope your aunt has provided enough neat's tongue for the two of us at supper tonight, eh?" She laughed heartily at her words, and Sophie smirked at her embarrassed cousin.

Letty flushed, hoping not too many people had overheard the duchess's comment. But to her deep mortification she saw that the person in line behind the duchess was the chestnut-haired gentleman she had seen in the park and at the dinner.

"Jules Wakeford, Marquess of Thornhill," she was informed. He met her eyes with a look of sardonic humor, and Letty flushed even more deeply. "Lord Wakeford," she said faintly.

"Charmed to make your acquaintance, Miss Biddle," he said.

Letty responded in form and turned away from him to the next person in line, his mother, the dowager countess, more quickly than was quite proper. Letty should have known the older woman was somehow related to the marquess, for she had the same thick chestnut hair, although hers was liberally streaked with gray. The dowager countess acknowledged Letty's presentation to her kindly, and Letty was next presented to her daughter, Lady Wakeford. The marquess's sister also had a strong family resemblance, but Letty was relieved to see his sister's eyes did not hold the same supercilious amusement when she looked at Letty. Indeed, Lady Wakeford seemed quite friendly, and Letty wished her cousin might have been more like her.

Most of the others Letty was presented to that evening blurred together in her mind, with one exception. That was Lord Satre, an older man with black hair streaked with gray, dressed immaculately in black silk breeches, ruffled silk shirt, a white waistcoat, and black coat. The lack of color in his clothes made his attire conspicuous. He was undeniably handsome and exquisitely polite, yet the look he directed at Letty made her feel uncomfortable. *Unclean* was a better word, she decided. He looked at her as though she stood in the receiving line in nothing but her shift. She hoped she would not encounter him often in Society.

At last Lady Hardwick allowed Letty and Sophie to leave their positions at the door and begin the dancing. According to etiquette, the girls making their come-out danced first with ranking gentlemen present. Sophie, who ranked higher than Letty since she was the daughter of a baron, danced with Lord Satre, and Letty, to her horror, found herself required to dance with the supercilious Lord Wakeford. As he led her onto the floor, Letty thought dismally that since she always seemed to make some social error when she was around Lord Wakeford, she would probably trip or step on his immaculately shined shoes. To her great relief, she did not. Indeed, had it not been for the light of sardonic amusement always visible in his eyes, she would have enjoyed the dance very much. He was an excellent dancer, and Letty was graceful and light on her feet. When the dance was over he returned Letty to Lady Hardwick, where she was immediately claimed for the next dance by a handsome young man with brown hair. He was followed by another handsome young gentleman, and to her surprise Letty found herself much in demand.

Jules Wakeford watched Miss Biddle dance gracefully across the floor with Lord Arlington, feeling a sense of disappointment. After his first two encounters with Miss Biddle at the dinner and the park, he had counted on the heiress providing him with a continual source for amusing anecdotes with which to regale his friends at White's. The Beau had been most diverted by the stories of the neat's tongue and the red cape. But so far this night she had not fulfilled his hopes. Perhaps this Season would turn out as dull as the last. He gave an imperceptible shrug and went to find his partner for the dinner dance, Miss Frost, a pretty blonde.

When they went down to the supper room, Miss Frost asked Jules if they could join the group that contained her friend Miss Hardwick. Seeing that the group also contained Miss Biddle, Jules acquiesced and went to fill a plate for his partner. As they ate their dinner, the girls chattered inconsequently, and their partners, callow young youths, were so intimidated by the presence of the nonpareil Lord Wakeford at their table that they said very little at all. Jules's mind began to wander.

"Did you notice Mr. Addison's coat?" one of the girls, Miss Alcock, asked her friends. "He looks quite the popinjay in that coat with the padded shoulders and small tails," she proclaimed, looking at the exquisite young gentleman in a bright yellow coat.

"Yes, and with lavender breeches," Miss Biddle's voice chimed in.

Jules's wandering attention was reclaimed. Young ladies did not use the word "breeches." Her comment caused an uncomfortable silence to fall at the table. The men looked embarrassed, and Miss Frost tittered.

"Miss Biddle," Miss Alcock dared to explain to Letty in a low voice as the silence lengthened, "a young lady does not refer to a gentleman's, ah, nether garment, with that word. One refers to them as 'inexpressibles,' 'ineffables,' or perhaps 'unmentionables.' "

Jules saw Miss Biddle's delicate face turn red with embarrassment at her faux pas. He glanced at her cousin and saw a strange look cross Miss Hardwick's face, composed of mortification and malicious pleasure.

"You must forgive my cousin," Miss Hardwick said to the group. "She is from the country and not accustomed to town manners. In Derbyshire I suppose a certain coarseness of expression is not minded."

Miss Alcock's supper partner, Lord Rutherford, kindly turned the subject, and the moment passed. Jules smiled to himself. Miss Biddle had not let him down after all.

* * *

Letty's blunder at supper shook her confidence, particularly since her comment had been overheard by Lord Wakeford, but by the end of the evening she had regained her spirits. She had not sat out a single dance. The gentlemen, excepting Lord Wakeford, had all been quite kind and did not seem to mind that she was newly come up to London from the country.

Lady Hardwick turned to her daughter and niece with satisfaction as the last of the guests departed. "I am most pleased with the way the evening went," she proclaimed. "It was a definite success. You did quite well, Laetitia," she unbent to say to her niece. "I did not notice any mistakes on your part."

"That is not quite true, Mama," Sophie contradicted, and proceeded to recount the supper conversation to her mother. Lady Hardwick frowned, but did not seem too upset by the incident.

"You must watch yourself very carefully, Laetitia" was all she said. "Refinement in one's conversation is expected of a young lady in London." Lady Hardwick was feeling quite benevolent toward her niece. She recognized that it was the lure of her fortune that had persuaded so many titled gentlemen to attend. And not only gentlemen. The dowager countess of Wakeford had come, as well as the Duchess of Grimwold. Never before had such exalted personages crossed the threshold of their house.

Sophie saw her mother's softening toward her cousin and resented it. She had had no lack of partners herself, but it made her jealous to see her cousin have any success in Society at all. She felt it was time to put her cousin in her place.

"Perhaps you ought to warn Cousin Letty about fortune hunters now that she has been presented to Society," she said with false concern. "Many of the gentlemen who danced with you tonight are short of funds and hope to ingratiate themselves with you in hope of gaining control of your fortune. I do not have to worry about such considerations," she added. "Gentlemen who dance with me do so because they wish to, not because of my wealth."

Sophie's unkind words robbed the evening of some of its pleasure to Letty. She looked at her aunt appealingly.

"There is truth in what Sophie says," Lady Hardwick acknowledged. "You will indeed have to be on your guard against fortune hunters. I have put it about that your father has control of your fortune until you are of age, but that will not keep all of them away. Do not worry, we shall find you an acceptable match anyway."

Letty went down slowly to her room. Was what Sophie had said true? Was it because of her fortune that so many gentlemen sought her out, and not because they found her likable or attractive? When she had first come to London, she had not paid much heed to her aunt's constant references to her as an heiress, but now she remembered it. Was that why she was being accepted into the *haut ton,* despite the fact she was only a squire's daughter? She had never really thought about the extent of her fortune and its affect on others, but she did now, and the idea that she was accepted only because of it was very disquieting.

Chapter Four

The next morning, the men who had danced with Letty and Sophie at their come-out the night before made their obligatory calls to Adam Street, stopping for a short visit or leaving their cards and flowers. The girls sat with Lady Hardwick in the Grand Salon to receive their visitors. Sophie, dressed in pale blue muslin, appeared unusually animated and attractive. In contrast, Letty's naturally high spirits were subdued, and she felt as colorless as the drab beige dress she wore. She found herself looking at the young men who came to call on her with a suspicion that made her feel uncomfortable but which she could not shake. Sophie's words of the night before made her doubt their sincerity. Did the gentlemen like her for herself, or were they only thinking of her fifty thousand pounds? Her suspicions made her reply to their conversational efforts in monosyllables, and they soon turned their attention to the more receptive Sophie. Letty noticed this and looked at her cousin almost enviously. What Sophie had said the night before was true. Her cousin had no worries. Sophie had only a modest fortune, not enough to interest a fortune hunter. Those who were gallant to her must be gallant for her own sake. Right now she was smiling up at Mr. Eastman, a handsome young man with blond hair, dressed in a pink coat and pea-green pantaloons, who had paid Sophie particular attention the night before.

Lady Hardwick frowned meaningfully at Letty when she failed to make a response to a remark addressed to her by Lord Arlington, and Letty roused herself to make an effort to speak to the young man doggedly trying to converse with her. At least, Letty thought, she had been spared the necessity of trying to speak with the supercilious Lord Wakeford. He had left flowers, but had not stayed.

As the morning wore on, the stream of callers decreased, and in the early afternoon Letty was able to escape from the Grand Salon to her small room behind the library. She was beginning to suspect she had been placed there to be out of the way of her aunt and cousin, whose bedchambers were on the first floor, but she was just as glad. Sophie had continually rejected her overtures of friendship, and Lady Hardwick did not seem overly eager for her niece's company either.

Letty wrote another letter home to her parents, telling them of the success of the come-out ball. Then, feeling a need to escape the town house, she rang for Daisy. They would go for a walk. She asked Daisy to get out her new walking dress, pelisse, and walking shoes. She would not again make the mistake of going out unaccompanied or dressed improperly.

A few minutes later she checked her reflection in the looking-glass. The now-familiar dissatisfaction with her appearance in her new clothes pricked at her. She could not deny that the walking dress with its tiny rows of tucks and pleats at the hem was in the latest fashion, but the muted green color did little for her complexion, and the brown pelisse with matching brown fringe was downright dull. It crossed her mind that it was possible her aunt had purposely selected styles and colors that were less than flattering on her, but she quickly dismissed the thought as unkind and ungrateful. Her aunt was used to dressing Sophie, and the styles that flattered one of Sophie's plump looks were not as suitable for her slender frame, that was all. Perhaps, she thought, she could find an attractive hat in the shops this afternoon and purchase it.

That idea made Letty more cheerful, and she and Daisy stepped out for their walk briskly. In a few minutes they arrived in Bond Street, and slowed to look at the inviting displays in the shop windows. Absorbed in the displays, Letty did not notice that there were few women in the street, and that those who were out were of a certain class. Nor did she notice the looks she was receiving from the men who walked and rode by. She saw a wide-brimmed hat trimmed in red that she liked in a milliner's, and she and Daisy entered the shop.

The proprietress looked with surprise at her customer, who was obviously a young lady, and wondered how she came to be out by herself in Bond Street in the afternoon. Perhaps she only looked innocent, she decided, and called an assistant to serve the young customer.

Letty whiled away a pleasant half hour trying on hats, delighted to see how much more becoming to her they were than the deep-brimmed bonnets of straw her aunt had selected. She eliminated all but a bonnet of twist with a short lace veil and the wide-brimmed Gypsy hat she had seen in the window. Feeling a little guilty, she asked the assistant to pack both. Letty thought regretfully that she could not purchase too much, or it would appear that she did not like her aunt's choice in her clothes. The shop girl handed the boxes to Daisy to carry, and they exited the shop.

Now that she had made the purchase she wanted, Letty looked around the street a bit more, and became aware that there were few women about and that the men looked at her in a bold manner that made her uncomfortable. She was beginning to feel that perhaps she should return home, when she heard a voice behind her.

"Miss Biddle. Good afternoon."

"Lord Wakeford," Letty acknowledged reluctantly, stopping to speak as manners dictated she must. As she turned and reluctantly met his eyes, she saw that they held the glint of amusement they always seemed to have when he looked at her. It was a pity he was so top-lofty, she thought wistfully, for there was no denying he was a very well-looking gentleman. His blue superfine morning coat and tight pantaloons outlined a trim form, and with his beaver and walking stick he looked complete to a shade. Perhaps she would have liked him better if she did not always have the feeling that the amusement in his eyes was directed at *her*.

"Shopping, I see," he said, indicating the boxes

in Daisy's arms. "Do Lady Hardwick and Miss Hardwick accompany you?"

"No. They were still abed when I left."

Jules hesitated. Should he say anything? The chit obviously did not know that ladies did not shop Bond Street in the afternoon. Only women of the *demi-monde* did so. He was finding her social blunders most diverting, but he could not wish any young woman of good family to be labeled fast. A brief glance up the street told him that her presence had attracted attention, and he decided to venture a warning.

"Miss Biddle, perhaps you are not aware it is not the thing to shop Bond Street in the afternoon."

Letty's eyes opened wide. "My maid is with me."

"No matter. Ladies shop Bond Street only in the morning. To be seen walking in Bond Street in the afternoon, even if accompanied by a maid, marks one as fast."

Letty flushed. This superior-looking beau always seemed to catch her in social errors.

"Thank you," she said stiffly. "I was not aware. My aunt only told me I must not go out unaccompanied."

"No doubt it did not occur to her that a girl from Derbyshire would not be aware of town customs. If I were you," he added kindly, "I should not go anywhere without first telling Lady Hardwick where you plan to go so she can tell you if it is acceptable or not."

"No doubt you are correct," Letty said, her mortification increasing. "Thank you for your warning, Lord Wakeford. I had best return home, then," she finished, and with an inclination of her head walked rapidly down the street, Daisy trotting behind.

Jules stood a moment, watching her rapid disappearance down the street with a smile. The chit was quite out of her depth in town. Even her maid, with her bright red hair and freckles, proclaimed that she hailed from the country. What did Miss Biddle hope to achieve by coming to London for the Season? To find a husband, he supposed. No doubt her parents had thought her fortune would enable her to make a good catch. For his own sake he was glad she had come, for her presence in Society promised to enliven the Season greatly.

Letty hoped to escape to her room unnoticed when she reached home, wishing to keep her latest blunder from her aunt, but the footman who opened the door informed her that her aunt had requested her immediate presence in the Grand Salon when she returned. Letty gave him her pelisse and went upstairs reluctantly, hoping she would be able to avoid telling her aunt of her latest error. She paused momentarily at the door. Her aunt was relaxing in a wing-back chair, and Sophie was sitting nearby, working on some embroidery.

"Where have you been, Laetitia?" Lady Hardwick demanded, becoming aware of Letty's presence in the doorway.

Letty advanced into the room reluctantly. "I went shopping with Daisy," she replied, hoping her aunt would not pursue the subject any further.

"Where?" Lady Hardwick inquired, dousing Letty's hopes.

"Bond Street," Letty replied truthfully, and noticed her cousin's head come up at her reply. Sophie ceased working on her embroidery and listened intently.

"Bond Street in the afternoon!" her aunt exclaimed in horrified accents. "Seen by everyone, no doubt."

"Lord Wakeford was the only person I saw whom I recognized," Letty protested feebly.

"Lord Wakeford, and others, no doubt, who recognized you if you did not recognize them. Although Lord Wakeford is enough by himself, since he is an intimate of Beau Brummell. Lady Hardwick shook her head in exasperation. "What am I to do with you, Laetitia? You make social errors one after the other. One would think you had no idea at all of how to behave in polite society. I must get you married off before all Society gets a disgust of you despite your fortune. Please remember that your behavior also reflects upon me and your cousin. We are, after all, responsible for you while you are residing with us."

Letty hung her head and shifted her feet uncomfortably as she stood before her aunt. Her aunt's words hurt, yet she understood the shame Lady Hardwick must have felt at being disgraced, albeit unintentionally, by her niece.

"I am sorry, Aunt. I shall try harder," she promised, thinking that these words seemed to be the ones she most often spoke to her aunt. She *did* mean to try, and she *was* sorry. It was just that no matter how hard she tried, she seemed to fail.

"Well, it is to be expected, I suppose, in one of your provincial upbringing," her aunt replied in a resigned voice. "Let us hope the harm is not irreparable.

"I had originally requested your presence to inform you that we shall be attending several routs tonight, after dinner at Lord Eastman's. I am glad that is all I had planned, for I doubt that even you can make a social gaffe at a rout, and I hope you learned from your first experience at dinner how to behave at one. Please display more animation than you have been when in company. A long face at the table ruins one's digestion. Speak to your neighbors, and do not forget to offer the dishes placed before you to those next to you."

"Yes, Aunt," Letty replied, and asked to be excused to rest awhile. She only hoped, she thought as she went downstairs to her room, that her aunt was correct about her not being able to make a mistake at a rout, whatever that was. She had never attended one and did not know what one was, but had been reluctant to confess her ignorance to her relatives. They were already disgusted with her lack of social knowledge.

Letty dressed carefully for the evening's entertainment in a fitted frock of pale apricot and wore her carnelians. She was determined to acquit herself well that evening. During the carriage ride to the Eastmans' town house that night, she felt a tightness developing in her chest. Social engagements were becoming ordeals. When she had first arrived in London, she had looked forward to having new experiences, but now she was beginning to dread them. She was sure that somehow she would make a mistake, no matter how hard she tried not to.

At the dining table Letty found herself seated between Lord Satre and Lord Arlington, a pleasant young man Letty remembered from her come-out ball. She spoke briefly to both, and applied herself to the soup. As the dinner progressed, she was careful to offer the dishes before her to her neighbors and not to eat too much of any one. Remembering her aunt's admonition to be more animated, she felt she must speak again to her neighbors, and glanced at them nervously. She did not wish to speak to Lord Satre, who made her feel uncomfortable, and Lord Arlington was conversing with the young woman seated at his other side.

Letty looked across the table, and recognized Lord Rutherford, a suitor of one of Sophie's friends, seated opposite. Seeing he was not involved in conversation, she addressed a remark to him. To her discomfiture, his eyes widened in apparent surprise at her words, and the guests in their immediate vicinity looked at her curiously. Lord Rutherford responded briefly to her comment and then pointedly addressed himself to the woman on his left. Letty flinched and felt ready to cry at this mild cut, knowing that somehow she must have committed another social solecism, although what it could possibly have been she did not know. Surely a question about one's health did not constitute a blunder.

She glanced down the table to her aunt and cousin, hoping that whatever error she had made had passed unnoticed by them, but she was not so fortunate. Both were glaring at her fiercely, and, of course, there was Lord Wakeford next to Lady Hardwick, looking at her with that aggravating smile on his face. Letty directed her attention back to her plate and concentrated on her food, although her appetite was gone. She resigned herself to another tense evening and knew she would find out later in the carriage what she had done wrong.

As she expected, her aunt began scolding her as soon as the carriage door closed.

"Whatever possessed you to converse *across* the table at dinner, Laetitia?"

Letty was bewildered. Was *that* it? "Is it wrong to converse across the table?"

"When one is dining at a small table with family or close friends it is acceptable, but not at a formal meal. One converses only with one's partners on the immediate right and left. Imagine how loud it would be if everyone raised their voices to converse across and down the table."

"I was quite shamed in front of Mr. Eastman," Sophie interjected. "Must Letty go with us everywhere?"

"She would not make as many mistakes if you did as I requested and instructed her in the proper behavior," Lady Hardwick said more sharply than she usually spoke to her daughter. Her niece's constant social blunders might be making it appear that she was not doing her duty. She could just imagine what Lady Upton was saying about her on her morning calls.

"I did my best, Mama," Sophie began to reply angrily, but Lady Hardwick motioned her to silence and addressed her niece again.

"At least, as I said before, I doubt that you can make a spectacle of yourself at a rout. That is a blessing, for we have three to attend tonight, beginning with one at the Duchess of Grimwold's."

Letty wondered again what a rout was, but she did not dare to ask. She only hoped her aunt was correct in thinking that she could not make a mistake at one. She sighed inaudibly. It seemed to her that her aunt made too much of what were minor infractions of the rules, surely. Perhaps in London people attached more importance to following all the rules to the letter.

When they arrived at the duchess's residence, it was close to eleven. A great crush of carriages was before the house, and seeing the huge residence lit with thousands of candles brought back memories to Letty of her first disgrace in the eyes of London Society the night she had eaten all the neat's tongues. Her nervousness returned, and by the time their carriage completed its excruciatingly slow progress to the door a half hour later, she could feel that her palms were damp and her heart racing. Again a footman in elaborate livery opened their carriage door with a flourish, and they joined the crush of people making its way into the great house. They moved slowly up the veined marble stairs to a large salon, where the duchess greeted her guests briefly. To Letty's relief, this time the duchess made no reference to their first meeting.

They passed through the salon into an adjoining room and on through an entire suite of rooms. Letty wondered what the planned amusement was, for she saw no cards or food, and heard no music. They could hardly move, and the rooms were quite stifling with the heat of the candles and crowds of people. Letty stayed close to her aunt's skirts lest she lose her in the crush, when suddenly she found they were back outside and waiting for their carriage.

Letty was confused. She could not help asking as she got into the carriage, "What is the purpose of a rout, Aunt Henrietta?"

"Purpose?" Lady Hardwick repeated, smoothing her silk skirts and adjusting her headdress.

"There was no food, nor did I see any rooms prepared for cards or dancing."

Sophie sniggered at this new evidence of her cousin's stupidity. "The purpose is to be seen," she informed Letty loftily. "For people to notice we were there. They will tell others, and we shall receive more invitations to better entertainments."

"I see," Letty replied, although she did not. To her it seemed a waste of time. But at least her aunt was correct that it was impossible for her to make a mistake at one.

The next rout they were attending was at Lord and Lady Perth's. The young couple's London house had just been completed, and they wished to show it off to Society. The first room of the suite they had opened for the rout was fairly commonplace, but as Letty and her aunt and cousin moved slowly into the second drawing room, she drew in her breath with wonder. The room seemed to go on forever, and to be filled with thousands of guests dressed in bright silks and glittering jewels. She wondered at the size of the room until she realized it was an illusion created by the walls being covered with mirrors. But the sensation of being in an immense room with thousands of people continued to persist. The great chandeliers, the jewels adorning the guests, and even the silk and satin gowns of the guests reflected the light of the hundreds of candles, and the mirrors intensified and multiplied the effect. Letty began to feel disoriented, and she could not focus on any one shape or person. Everything seemed to swirl together in one mass of light and color, and Letty realized to her dismay that she was going to faint. She reached out to clutch her aunt's skirts, and then everything vanished.

Letty opened her eyes to a burning sensation in her nose. She choked and turned her head away from the bottle of smelling salts her cousin held too closely under her nose.

"She has come around," she heard her aunt say as from a great distance.

"Yes, I think she will be all right," a familiar voice replied.

Letty recognized the voice as Lord Satre's, and tried to sit up. Her aunt came and stood over her.

"You owe thanks to Lord Satre," her aunt said. "He was nearby when you were overcome by the heat and carried you to this room."

Letty thanked Lord Satre for his assistance, but the idea of having been carried in his arms was distasteful to her. She saw a strange light in his eyes and shuddered involuntarily. Lady Hardwick saw the tremor, and assumed it was caused by her weakness.

"Are you able to walk to the carriage?" she asked.

"I shall assist her," Lord Satre volunteered.

"No, I am quite able to walk," Letty protested, standing up, but Lord Satre insisted on putting his arm around her shoulder as he escorted her from the house and out to the carriage. Letty disliked his touch and tried to pull away, but he only held her nearer. She was relieved when they reached the carriage and he was forced to release her. As she settled back on the squabs, her aunt thanked Lord Satre once more for his assistance and gave the driver instructions to take them home. They would have to miss the third rout she had planned to attend. Letty felt miserable with the knowledge that she had managed to disgrace herself yet again, and rode home silently. When they arrived back at Adam Street she apologized to her aunt and went slowly to her room.

"Did you have a good time this evening, miss?" Daisy asked as she helped Letty out of her evening clothes.

"It was pleasant," Letty replied evasively, not wishing to go into details.

"Daisy," she said suddenly as she placed her simple carnelian necklace back into her jewel-case, "has London lived up to your expectations?"

"*My* expectations, miss?" Daisy asked, surprised, as she unfastened her mistress's gown.

"Yes," Letty replied as she stepped from the gown. "Is London what you thought it would be before we came?"

"Well, miss," Daisy replied, "to be truthful, it isn't quite as exciting as I had hoped." She did not expand to tell her mistress of her dreams of a handsome London footman who would take her about and show her a good time. While the servants at the Hardwicks' town house were not exactly unkind, they had let her know how superior they were to a country maid.

"I do not find it so either," Letty said, slipping between the warmed sheets of her bed. "I suppose that is what Papa and Mama tried to warn me about when I first asked to have a London Season."

Letty felt a sharp pang of homesickness at the thought of her mother and father. *They* had never been so harsh and critical of her behavior. She sighed aloud as Daisy folded her gown away. "Perhaps it will get better. We have been here only two weeks."

"Perhaps, miss," Daisy repeated doubtfully as she extinguished the candles.

The next day was Wednesday, and Sophie had the pleasure of informing her cousin that while *she* would be attending the assembly at Almack's that evening, Letty would not.

"For your father is only a squire, and although you may have a fortune, it has the taint of trade," she explained condescendingly. "Only those of the best *ton* are granted vouchers to Almack's."

Letty felt disappointed at this news, for she had heard of Almack's even in Derbyshire. It surprised her, too, that her aunt and cousin would attend and leave her alone for the evening.

"Sophie was granted vouchers before you arrived," Lady Hardwick explained. "I know you would not wish Sophie to miss out on attending because you cannot go."

"Of course not, Aunt Henrietta," Letty replied.

Letty could not help feel a little sorry for herself that evening when Sophie and Lady Hardwick departed for the famous assembly rooms. She scolded herself and spent the evening reading one of the books Sophie had gotten at the circulating library. The evening was surprisingly pleasant, and she was able to greet her cousin with equanimity when she returned, full of her success at the rooms. Letty consoled herself that she would be going to the ball tomorrow night at the Rutherfords'.

The ball the next night did much to restore her spirits. Letty had decided not to worry about whether her partners were interested in her for her fortune and just to enjoy the dancing. Dancing, at least, was one thing she could do well. She had no lack of partners, and the gentlemen were very charming and complimentary. Even Lord Wakeford, who claimed her third dance, did not display his usual mocking smile. Miss Alcock and Miss Frost, two of Sophie's friends, spoke to her, and pointed out the famous Beau Brummell, who was in attendance.

After a long country dance, Letty stood alone a moment at the edge of the floor, trying to catch her breath before the next dance, when she saw Lord Satre approaching. Letty felt her heart sink at the thought of having to dance with Lord Satre. Although he was impeccably well mannered and well dressed, still there was something indefinable about him she could not like. The thought of his arms about her the night she had fainted made her skin crawl with distaste, and she determined to avoid dancing with him if she could.

"Miss Biddle," he said with a polished bow and smile, "may I solicit the pleasure of your hand for the next dance?"

"Thank you, Lord Satre," Letty replied, "but I am fatigued and would prefer to sit this one out."

"Then allow me to bear you company.

"I would not presume to keep you from the pleasure of dancing with another lady not so fatigued," Letty said awkwardly. The idea of sitting next to him and talking while his eyes devoured her was as abhorrent as the idea of dancing with him.

An almost imperceptible widening of Lord Satre's eyes indicated his surprise at her refusal, which constituted a blatant cut. Astonished and inwardly furious that a chit from the country dared refuse him, he was too polished to let it show.

"Another time, then, Miss Biddle," he said mildly, and left with another bow.

Letty, unaware of the magnitude of the insult she had just dealt Lord Satre, breathed with relief as he led another woman onto the floor. Lord Arlington, who had been out of the ballroom and had missed Letty's refusal of Lord Satre, saw that Letty did not have a partner and asked her to dance with him. Letty accepted gratefully, happy to have escaped from an uncomfortable situation so easily.

* * *

Lord Wakeford, standing across the ballroom with Beau Brummell and his court, noticed the blatant cut Letty had given Lord Satre, as had most of the room.

"Who is the young girl who administered the shocking cut to Satre?" the Beau asked Lord Wakeford.

Jules smiled. "That is the provincial heiress I have been telling you about, Miss Biddle."

The Beau looked at Letty with heightened interest, remembering the amusing anecdotes Wakeford had regaled him with at White's the past two weeks.

"She is so ignorant of the ways of Polite Society that I doubt she knows she administered a cut by accepting the hand of another gentleman for a dance immediately after refusing Satre," Jules continued.

The Beau looked at Jules in amazement and then shook his head. "What can one expect of a girl from the country," he said as though that explained it all. "I never go there myself. It is much too barbarous. It is fortunate Miss Biddle is an heiress to great wealth, although even that would not tempt me to ally myself with such a rustic."

"Yes, she is quite socially inept," Jules agreed. "Clumsy as an ox," he added, continuing the comparison with country things. Then inspiration struck and he laughed aloud. "She loppets through Society. 'Loppeting Letty,'" he said to the Beau, recalling Miss Biddle's given name and coupling it with a word normally used to refer to awkward farm animals.

" 'Loppeting Letty,' " the Beau repeated, amused. "Quite apt, she is so socially clumsy. Although it is a pity in one of such fine face and form. 'Letty Loppet,' though, I think. One need not follow the rules of grammar so strictly when bestowing a sobriquet."

The members of the Beau's court applauded and laughed, repeating the nickname among themselves, and then going to circulate in the ballroom, being eager to be the first to inform their friends of this latest example of the wit of the Beau and his friend Lord Wakeford.

Lord Arlington escorted Letty to her aunt after their dance, and Lady Hardwick barely waited for him to be out of earshot before hissing angrily in her niece's ear.

"What did you mean by cutting a man of rank like Lord Satre? Do you wish to ruin us?"

"Cut?" Letty asked, surprised. "I only refused to dance with him."

"Yes, you refused to partner him and then immediately accepted another gentleman's hand for the same dance. If you refuse to dance with one gentleman, you must refuse all others that evening as well. To do otherwise is to be inexcusably rude."

"But I do not like Lord Satre, and did not wish to dance with him."

"It makes no difference whether you *like* a prospective dance partner or not. One need not like a person to dance with him. Or you could have sat out the dance with him and conversed. What is there not to like about Lord Satre? He is both titled and wealthy."

Letty made no response, recognizing the justice of her aunt's words. She had known she was being impolite to refuse to partner Lord Satre, yet she could not be sorry for it. However, she knew she would not be able to explain the strange, unclean feeling being in Lord Satre's presence engendered, and she remained silent.

"Fortunately, Lord Satre is disposed to allow for your youth and inexperience in the ways of Society," Lady Hardwick continued. "I apologized to him after the dance, and he is taking you for a ride in the park tomorrow afternoon. You will not insult him again."

Letty heard her aunt's words with dismay, but could think of no way to avoid the drive, and the appearance of Sophie and her partner prevented her making further protest.

Letty feared that her cut of Lord Satre would prevent her from having partners for the rest of the evening, but if anything, she seemed more popular than ever. Yet it seemed to her that many of the gentlemen looked at her strangely, with smiles that mirrored the amused one she had so often seen on Lord Wakeford's lips when he was in her company. No, she scolded herself, she was becoming too self-conscious because of her mistakes and reading too much into people's expressions.

She had not gotten wind of the nickname that had been bestowed upon her that evening.

Chapter Five

The morning after the ball at the Rutherfords', Jules went down to the breakfast room at his usual hour of seven and was surprised to find his sister there before him. He always rose early in order to enjoy a ride in the near-empty park, but Emily and his mother rarely rose before ten during the Season.

"To what do I owe the pleasure of your company so early this morning, sister?" he inquired as he poured a cup of coffee and helped himself to some kidneys and rashers from the covered dishes on the sideboard.

His sister waited until he had filled his plate and seated himself across from her before setting down her cup of chocolate and answering his question.

"I thought the breakfast room would be a private place in which to give you the scold you deserve."

Jules smiled indulgently. "What have I done to earn a scold from you?"

"I heard of the nickname Miss Biddle was given last night, and I suspect you are the one who bestowed it upon her," Emily said frankly.

"I confess," Jules said lightly, finishing a rasher and turning his attention to the kidney. "It came to me as I was conversing with the Beau. He had been

70

speaking of the country, and her ungainly social behavior reminded me of a clumsy farm animal. My remark was overheard and spread about."

Emily looked at her brother disapprovingly. "You look pleased with yourself. I think it was a very unkind thing to do. Imagine how Miss Biddle must feel to be so labeled."

"Save your pity for those more deserving of it, sister dear," Jules advised. "One as wealthy as Miss Biddle can do nothing that will put her out of favor with Society."

Emily frowned at her brother in real displeasure. "Her wealth does not mean she cannot be hurt by such a nickname being attached to her," she admonished. "When I met her at her come-out ball, I quite liked her. She appeared to be a good-hearted and unaffected girl. You have often complained about the usual simpering Society misses. Yet here is a girl who is not one, and all you can do is make her a figure of fun to the Beau and his set. It is not well done of you."

Emily paused a moment and then resumed thoughtfully. "I think Miss Biddle cannot be very comfortable with her aunt and cousin. I never cared for Lady Hardwick and her daughter, and it appeared to me they treat Miss Biddle with indifference, if not actual unkindness. I rather suspect Lady Hardwick of agreeing to sponsor her because of the doors Miss Biddle's wealth would open to them. Lady Hardwick is only the widow of a baron."

Jules's first reaction to his sister's dressing down was irritation that his younger sister dared read him a scold, but the justice of her remarks prevented him from making the cutting rejoinder he wished. It was true he had not considered Miss Biddle's feelings. If anything, he had assumed that one of her wealth would be invulnerable to Society's scorn. He had watched with interest her debut into the world of the *haut ton* since the dinner at the Duchess of Grimwold's, deriving amusement from the blunders she made as she attempted to find her feet in a milieu that was totally foreign to her. He had not meant to be unkind. *Could* he have hurt her? His conscience awoke and pricked at him uncomfortably.

"I am sorry, Emily, if I caused Miss Biddle any pain or embarrassment, but there is little I can do about it now."

"Yes, there is," Emily contradicted him. "You can avoid referring to her as 'Letty Loppet,' and you can be seen in her company. If those gentlemen who know you gave her the nickname see you seek her out, they will know you were only being facetious, and have no real disgust of her company."

Jules's conscience went back to sleep. That was asking too much. He was truly sorry if he had caused Miss Biddle pain, but he was not going to be seen spending time in the company of such a provincial.

"Surely I need not go to such lengths," he protested, causing Emily's green eyes to flash angrily. "However, I shall not refer to her as 'Letty Loppet' again," he said to appease his sister.

Emily, however, was not satisfied with this concession. "I do not know what possessed you, Jules. You never used to be so unkind. And to someone who has done you no harm. I intend to befriend her whether you will or no."

With that, Emily got up from the table and swept from the room, her head held high and her sarcenet skirts whisking angrily about her feet.

Jules sat staring at the doorway through which his sister had passed, an expression of astonishment on his face. He had never seen Emily so upset with him. He was so used to admiration and unquestioning affection from his sister that it discomposed him to have her so angry with him. Perhaps she had a point, he admitted to himself reluctantly. He would ask the Biddle chit to go for a drive in the park one afternoon. That ought to satisfy Emily.

This resolution appeased his conscience, and his appetite returned. He got up from the table and helped himself to another kidney.

Neither Lady Hardwick nor Sophie had heard of Letty's nickname the night of the ball. No one would be so impolite as to tell them of it there. However, as soon as it was late enough to make a morning call, one of Lady Hardwick's acquaintances called to have the pleasure of informing her friend—for their own good, of course.

"It is fortunate your niece is so wealthy," Lady Upton said after the usual greetings had been exchanged and an offer of refreshment refused. "Such a sobriquet might be the death of all matrimonial hopes for a poorer girl." She smiled at Lady Hardwick with false commiseration.

Lady Hardwick had no idea what Lady Upton was speaking about, but suspected it was nothing good. However, she had no choice but to follow Lady Upton's conversational lead if she wished to find out. She gave her caller an inquiring look.

"You did not hear?" Lady Upton asked with patently false surprise. "But I suppose those who heard the nickname would hesitate to use it in your presence." She stopped a moment and looked about the ivory and gold room, prolonging her hostess's suspense. Before the silence stretched too long, she continued.

"One of the gentlemen, I am not sure who, gave Miss Biddle the appellation 'Letty Loppet' at the Rutherfords' ball last night. I believe it was in reference to her social clumsiness, perhaps after the incident with Lord Satre."

"Incident with Lord Satre?" Lady Hardwick asked innocently. "Whatever do you mean? You refer perhaps to his invitation to Laetitia to drive this afternoon?" At Lady Upton's look of surprise, Lady Hardwick knew she had scored a point. Now when Letty was seen with Lord Satre in the park that afternoon, it would minimize the damage done by her unfortunate behavior of the previous night.

"Gentlemen will have their amusement at the expense of the ladies," she continued, smiling and allowing none of her considerable dismay at the news of the nickname to show. "But as you say, one as wealthy as my niece need fear no loss of popularity. Nor one of her beauty, if you will forgive the natural pride of an aunt in saying so," she added.

"Of course," Lady Upton agreed, this last barb hitting home, since her daughter was not a beauty. In fact, the more unkind called her fox-faced. However, she was not yet routed.

"It is true it may not affect Miss Biddle's popularity," she granted. "You can only hope it does not affect your daughter's either." Wishing to retreat while she was ahead, Lady Upton rose to take her departure, leaving a dismayed Lady Hardwick behind.

As soon as she heard the sound of the front door

closing on her guest's back, Lady Hardwick gave the bell pull a sharp tug and told the footman who answered to have her niece and daughter attend her in the salon immediately.

Sophie, who had been in her bedchamber across the hall, came into the salon directly. "What is it, Mama?" she asked. Her mother did not answer, motioning her to sit. Letty came in a few minutes after her cousin, and started to sit next to her cousin, when her aunt prevented her.

"Come here, Laetitia," she said sternly, and Letty went to stand before her aunt.

"I regret to tell you," Lady Hardwick began, "that your provincial manners have brought the opprobrium of an unflattering sobriquet being attached to you. Lady Upton was pleased to inform me this morning that you have become known as 'Letty Loppet' to Society. A gentleman awarded you the name after seeing you cut Lord Satre last night.

"The nickname will probably do no lasting damage to you, but the notoriety that will be attached to us all is distasteful in the extreme."

Lady Hardwick paused for a breath. Her two listeners were hearing the news with very different reactions. Letty had turned red with mortification at hearing a word commonly used to describe clumsy farm animals being applied to her. A malicious smile of pleasure had crossed Sophie's face at the news. Lady Hardwick, observing the smile, momentarily turned her anger upon her daughter.

"This reflects not only upon Laetitia, but upon me as her sponsor and you as her cousin. In fact, miss, it is more likely to affect your prospects than Laetitia's, since you have no fortune to compensate."

This idea had not occurred to Sophie, and she looked at her cousin in resentment. "I do not see why her disgraceful behavior should affect me."

"It may be unjust, but that is the way of Society," Lady Hardwick proclaimed, and turned back to her niece. "I have tried to be understanding of your behavior, Laetitia, allowing for your being raised in the country, but you *must* make more of an effort. Surely you would not wish your cousin's prospects to be damaged by your behavior."

Letty, standing before her aunt in disgrace, felt conflicting emotions. Little as she got along with her cousin, still she did not want to be the cause of her not receiving a good offer. It was unfair of her aunt to say she had not tried. She *did* try. It just seemed no matter how hard she tried, she still made mistakes. She realized that the nickname explained the amused smiles she had seen on her partner's faces the night before. It had not been her imagination. She was a joke to them, yet they endured her presence because of her fortune. Suddenly she was overwhelmed with a desire to go home to Derbyshire, where she was accepted for what she was.

"Please, Aunt Henrietta," she burst out, "I wish to return to Derbyshire. Here I only bring down censure upon you and Sophie. Please allow me to go home," she begged.

The angry look left Sophie's face, and she seemed delighted at the idea of her cousin leaving. Lady Hardwick felt conflicting emotions at her niece's plea. She wished she might allow her niece to return to Derbyshire, but she had already spent a substantial part of the funds advanced to her by the squire, money she could not afford to repay. Besides, she needed Laetitia's presence in her home to open

76

doors that would otherwise remain closed to plain Miss Hardwick of no great fortune. The Season was not yet half over.

"What's this, miss?" she attacked her niece, rising from her chair and standing over Letty like a tartar. "You wish to return home? Ungrateful girl! How would that appear to my sister, who requested that I bring you out under my protection this Season? Have I not done my duty by you? Is it my fault you make blunder after blunder? I try my best. Do you wish to shame me further in the eyes of Society by leaving when the Season has barely begun? The answer is not for you to return home, but for you to make a greater effort to behave with propriety."

Letty felt her heart sink at the idea of staying. The Season would not be over for nearly six weeks. But there was some truth in her aunt's words. Lady Hardwick *had* taken on her presentation, and at Letty's own request. If Lady Hardwick and Sophie's welcome was not as warm as Letty had wished, was that sufficient reason for Letty to leave early? Her parents had tried to warn her, but she had insisted on coming to London. She doubted they would be receptive to her early return.

"Well, Laetitia?" her aunt demanded as the silence lengthened.

"You are correct, Aunt," Letty replied bleakly. "I promise to try harder in the future to behave in a manner that Society can find nothing to censure."

"I shall expect you to keep that promise," Lady Hardwick said. "Now go to your room and reflect upon the arrant ingratitude you have displayed."

Lady Hardwick waited until Letty had left the room and then sat back down.

"I can see you are not displeased by the nickname

that has been attached to Laetitia," she said to her daughter. "I advise *you* to think carefully about the fine line that divides what is detrimental to your cousin and what is detrimental to you as her close relative."

"Yes, Mama," Sophie answered, keeping her eyes downcast so that her mother would not divine her true feelings. It suited her quite well to have Letty ridiculed, and it angered her that her mother seemed suddenly disposed to side with her cousin over her own daughter. She intended to use the nickname to increase Society's disgust of her cousin, whatever her mother said.

Letty returned to her room and sat dejectedly on the graceful Chippendale window seat, staring miserably at the gray sky, tears filling her eyes as she thought of the nickname she had been given. How Society must despise her! This was not at all what she had dreamed a London Season would be like. She put her head in her hands and began to sob quietly, longing for her home and the unquestioning love of her parents.

Daisy, coming in with an armful of freshly pressed clothes, dropped them onto a chair at the sight of her mistress's distress and knelt beside her.

"What is the matter, Miss Letty?" she asked, her freckled face showing sympathy.

Daisy's compassion only made Letty cry harder. Between sobs she told of the nickname she had been given and her aunt's refusal to allow her to return to Derbyshire. Daisy, muttering soothing words, coaxed Letty to lie on her bed, and gently bathed her temples with lavender water. Letty's sobs ceased at her maid's kind ministrations, but she felt she could never go anywhere in London again, knowing what people were calling her behind her back.

An hour or so later, a knock sounded at the door and a servant told Daisy, Sophie wished her cousin to accompany her to the circulating library. Letty, waking from a light sleep, refused, pleading indisposition. She had seen her cousin's pleasure at her disgrace, and had no desire to go anywhere with Sophie.

Shortly after the maid carried her refusal to Sophie, Lady Hardwick appeared at Letty's door.

"What is this I hear of you refusing to accompany your cousin to the library?" she demanded without preamble.

"I am not feeling well, Aunt Henrietta," Letty explained, rising slowly from her bed at her aunt's entrance.

"Is it that or is it you do not wish to appear in public after hearing of the nickname?" her aunt asked perceptively. "That is precisely why you must go. You must behave as though the nickname has no effect on you.

"Get your mistress's pelisse and walking shoes out," Henrietta directed Daisy, and remained in the room until Letty was prepared to go.

"The walk will do you good and make you look more presentable for your drive this afternoon with Lord Satre."

Letty had not thought she could feel worse than she did, but her aunt's reminder about the drive with Lord Satre had that effect. Perhaps, she thought hopefully, if he had heard of her nickname, he would not come.

* * *

After a silent walk to the library, Letty took a chair near the doorway and waited while her cousin went to the counter and discussed just-published books with the clerk. She was staring fixedly into space, trying to be invisible and hoping no one she knew would come into the library while she was there, when a voice penetrated her consciousness.

"Do you not care for reading, Miss Biddle?"

Letty looked up to see a handsome young man in flawless morning dress standing before her. She did not recognize him, although evidently he knew who she was. She had probably been introduced to him and forgotten, she thought in despair. There were so *many* people she had met, she could not remember them all. But she thought she would have remembered such a handsome gentleman. She admired the picture he presented in his blue coat with gilt buttons, buff breeches, shining Hessians, and blond hair carefully arranged *à la* Titus. She hesitated, unsure what to do since she could not remember his name.

He smiled in understanding of her predicament and swept her a bow. "Viscount Courtney, at your service."

Letty returned the smile, deciding she liked him, and answered his earlier question. "Yes, I like to read, Lord Courtney, but I generally allow my cousin to select the books. I am not familiar with the popular authors."

"Allow me to assist you in making a choice," Lord Courtney offered, holding out his arm. Letty glanced briefly at Sophie, catching her eye, and then allowed Lord Courtney to escort her to the counter opposite the one where her cousin stood.

80

"What author's books does your cousin customarily borrow?" Lord Courtney questioned.

"Mrs. Radcliffe's novels," Letty answered.

"Do you enjoy them?"

"Very much."

Her response seemed to give Lord Courtney the information he needed.

"Get *Belinda* for Miss Biddle to inspect, if you please," he instructed the clerk.

"If you enjoy Mrs. Radcliffe's books, I think you will enjoy Mrs. Edgeworth's even more," he said to Letty as the clerk found the book he had requested and handed it to Letty.

As Letty leafed interestedly through the book, Sophie picked up her selections and joined her cousin.

"It is time we leave, Letty," she said abruptly.

Letty looked up at her cousin in surprise. "First I would like to borrow this book," she said, holding it out to Sophie.

"You do not have a subscription and I do not have time to wait for you to get one," Sophie said impatiently, taking the volume from her cousin and handing it back to the clerk. "You can get it another time."

Reluctantly Letty turned to follow her cousin as Sophie hastened from the store, thanking Lord Courtney with a smile.

She and Sophie had gone only a few yards down the street when Letty heard quick footsteps behind them and Lord Courtney caught up with the girls.

"Miss Biddle," he said, holding out a volume. "I took the liberty of getting *Belinda* for you on my subscription. I know one is not supposed to get books for another on one's own subscription, but I trust you to take care of it and hope you will allow me to come and pay a call on you next week to retrieve the volume."

Letty took the volume with a smile. "Thank you, Lord Courtney. I should be pleased if you would call," she answered, ignoring Sophie's fierce frown.

Lord Courtney smiled and took his leave of the two girls, smiling at Sophie's determined snubbing.

"What do you mean by speaking to a man to whom you have not been introduced? I shall have to inform Mama."

"He knew who I was, and he is undoubtedly a gentleman," Letty protested. "How do you know I have not been introduced to him?"

"I know because although I have not been introduced to him either, I know who he is. You could not have met him before, because he has not been in town. It makes no difference that he is a gentleman. To speak to any man to whom you have not been previously introduced makes one look fast."

Letty was silent. Of course, she should have known. She could not even manage a short trip to the library without committing some kind of social error. But to her surprise she found she did not care, since it had been the means of meeting Lord Courtney. He was the first man she had met who she did not feel looked down on her as being a lesser person because she was from the country.

"You may tell your mother if you please," Letty said daringly, "but if you do, I shall tell her that you saw him speaking to me in the library and made no attempt to inform me it was wrong until it was too late."

Sophie looked surprised and displeased at Letty's defiance, and they walked home in an angry silence.

Even the ride Lady Hardwick had accepted for Letty with Lord Satre that afternoon did not have the power to dim Letty's rise of spirits at her meeting with Lord Courtney. As Lord Satre helped her into his glossy black curricle and jumped in beside her, she even resolved to apologize for her impolite behavior the night before.

"I hope you will forgive me my refusal to dance with you last night," Letty said. "I had felt temporarily faint after the exertion of the long country dance, and wished to be alone for a moment to recover. I did not realize it was wrong of me to accept another partner when I had recovered," she continued, quite proud of herself for her likely sounding explanation. "I am only recently arrived in London from Derbyshire, and I fear I am not yet accustomed to all the rules of Society."

"There is no need to apologize, Miss Biddle, I quite understand," Lord Satre replied with a smile, looking directly into her eyes.

At his penetrating look, Letty's pride in her excuse vanished, and she had the uncomfortable feeling he did indeed understand only too well. His gray eyes seemed to have the power to read her very soul. She felt her face flush, and looked away, a shiver going down her spine. She pretended to admire the scenery in the park, and was grateful for the presence of the other carriages and riders. She would never care to be completely alone with Lord Satre.

They stopped several times to speak to acquaintances, and Letty noted their barely concealed surprise at seeing Letty in company with Lord Satre. Perhaps the ride would have a benefit after all, she thought, and prevent people from calling her Letty Loppet.

That night, as Letty dressed for another ball, she reflected on the difference in her feelings since she had first arrived in London barely three weeks earlier. Then she had thought her money a blessing because it enabled her to have a London Season. She had looked forward to attending glittering balls and being one with the *haut ton*. After her first social gaffes, each social occasion had seemed like a test which she usually failed. As recently as this morning, after hearing of the nickname, she had felt she never wished to appear in Society again. But now, after meeting Lord Courtney, she was actually looking forward to the ball, for *he* might be there.

She dressed with especial care, but as Daisy coaxed the final curl into place, Letty looked at her reflection with the familiar feeling of dissatisfaction. The sage-green color of the gown did nothing for her skin, and the close-fitting bodice made her figure appear childish.

"Somehow, Daisy," she said aloud, "the clothes Aunt Henrietta selected for me are just not becoming." Silently she wondered again if her aunt had chosen unflattering styles deliberately, but she could think of no reason for such an action.

"Maybe your necklace will help," Daisy suggested, opening Letty's meager jewel-case and holding the garnets about her throat. But the jewels did not look right with the sage-green color, nor did the carnelians, which were Letty's only other jewels.

"Neither of them looks well with this gown," Letty said. "I suppose I should purchase some new jewels, but it was one thing Aunt Henrietta did not suggest. I shall not wear any tonight," she decided.

Daisy returned the jewels to the case and got out Letty's brown velvet pelisse, shaking it and placing it around Letty's shoulders. Letty looked at the clock and hastened to the hall to join her aunt and cousin before they had to send for her.

When they arrived at the Arlingtons' town house, Letty entered behind her aunt and cousin, as was her custom. She handed her pelisse to a footman and joined her relatives, who were greeting Lord and Lady Arlington as they stood at the door of the ballroom. After speaking to Lady Hardwick and Sophie, Lady Arlington turned to Letty. A look of surprise, quickly masked, crossed her face, and for a terrible moment Letty thought something was wrong. But as Lady Arlingon expressed her pleasure at seeing her, Letty scolded herself for her fears. She must have imagined the look. She had become much too sensitive because of her past errors. She followed her aunt and Sophie to the gilt side chairs placed around the edge of the ballroom. Lady Hardwick glanced at Letty as she began to sit down, and then suddenly rose and stared at Letty in shock.

"Where are your jewels, Laetitia?" she demanded.

"I have only the garnets and carnelians and neither looked well with this gown," Laetitia explained, wondering why her aunt seemed so upset.

"Then you should have asked to borrow some from me or from Sophie. Don't you realize it is an insult to your hostess to appear at her home without being fully dressed? It implies you felt her entertainment was not worth your effort to prepare properly.

85

Well, it is too late to do anything now, since she has already seen you," Lady Hardwick said, a resigned tone to her voice. She sat down and shook her head at her niece. "I never thought to say it, but perhaps the nickname you were given was a good thing. What Lady Arlington would see as insult in another, she may forgive 'Letty Loppet.' "

Sophie smirked superiorly at Letty as she took a seat next to her mother, and Letty slowly took the chair at Lady Hardwick's other side. She looked glumly about the ballroom, her earlier excitement gone. She could do *nothing* right, she decided. And worse yet, she did not see Lord Courtney anywhere.

Mr. Eastman claimed Sophie for the opening set, and Letty accepted the hand of Sophie's other suitor, Lord Lockwood. She wondered, as she danced with him, what Sophie saw in Lord Lockwood. He was not handsome by any stretch of the imagination, and his manners were pompous and overbearing. Perhaps she just wished to have a second suitor in the wings in case Mr. Eastman did not come up to scratch.

Letty's second dance was claimed by her host's son, Lord Arlington, who was one of her most persistent suitors. Letty liked Lord Arlington, for he was one of the few she felt did not like her only because of her fortune, yet she had been very careful not to give him much encouragement. She had wondered at herself for not favoring one of her suitors over another, but this afternoon she had discovered why. None of them had caused her heart to race at the very sight of them, as hers had that afternoon when she met Lord Courtney. Lord Arlington returned her to her aunt at the end of the allemande, and to Letty's great delight, she saw Lord Courtney approaching. To her dismay, Lady Hardwick refused to allow Letty to dance with him, since they had not been formally introduced.

Lord Courtney was not so easily defeated, however, and returned shortly with Lady Arlington, who performed the requisite introductions, leaving Lady Hardwick with no choice but to allow Letty to dance with him.

"Your aunt is a high stickler," Lord Courtney commented as he led Letty onto the floor.

"Yes, and I fear I am a great trial to her," Letty confided. It suddenly occurred to her that perhaps Lord Courtney was being kind to her because he had been out of town and not heard of her reputation as a hopeless provincial. She determined to tell him herself. "I am not accustomed to the ways of London, being but recently arrived from Derbyshire. I am sure you have heard the sobriquet which has been attached to me. It was most mortifying to my aunt to have me so labeled."

Lord Courtney did not deny knowledge of her nickname. "Yes, I have heard of it, but I did not pay it any mind. I am sure you must misjudge your aunt's reaction, however. It would have been most unjust for her to blame you. It is only natural that you should take time to learn the ways of London Society, since you were not raised in them. You will learn with time."

"I have been here all of three weeks and have not learned them yet," Letty confessed. "There are so *many* rules one has to follow here in London. There are rules that guide one's behavior in the country, too, but not so many."

"To one not brought up in London it must be very difficult to remember them all," Lord Courtney sympathized. "If ever you are not sure of something, ask me. I have lived in London all my life."

Letty smiled at Lord Courtney gratefully, and then the dance separated them and conversation was not possible. Letty was glad that dancing was one thing she could do without disgracing anyone. She was very light on her feet and performed with a natural grace that was appreciated by all her partners. The long dance was rejuvenating, and she returned to her aunt with her spirits much restored.

Her next partner was Lord Wakeford. She was sure he noticed her lack of jewels, and was laughing at her behind his mask of politeness, but she refused to allow his mockery to cast down her spirits.

Although she did not enjoy her dance with Lord Wakeford, Letty was pleased when his sister, Lady Wakeford, came to pay her respects to Lady Hardwick and sat down to speak with her a few minutes. To Letty's delight, Lady Wakeford asked her to call upon her the next morning. How wonderful it would be to have a friend in London! She had met some of Sophie's friends, but they took their lead from her cousin and did not welcome Letty into their circle. She opened her mouth to accept the invitation, and then thought of Lord Wakeford. She hesitated, glancing involuntarily to where Lord Wakeford stood speaking to Lord Lockwood and Sophie.

Lady Wakeford followed the direction of her glance and laughed. "Jules will not be home, if that is why you hesitate, Miss Biddle."

Letty blushed at having her thoughts so easily read, and accepted Lady Wakeford's invitation.

In general the night went quite well, Letty decided, in spite of having had to dance twice with Lord Satre and once with Lord Wakeford. On the way home she sat in contented silence, thinking of Lord Courtney and the interest he was showing in her.

"Laetitia, it will not do for you to encourage Lord Courtney," her aunt broke into her thoughts, seemingly reading her mind.

Letty looked up in surprise. "Why not, Aunt Henrietta? He is a viscount, and is accepted in Society, or Lady Arlington would not have invited him to her ball and presented him to me as a suitable partner for a dance."

"Lord Courtney must be accepted in Society because of his rank," Lady Hardwick explained not unkindly, "but that does not make him eligible as a suitor. Lord Courtney is a known fortune hunter. He has already gone through what he inherited from his father, and needs to find a rich wife before his creditors lose patience and have him thrown in Newgate."

Letty heard her aunt's words with a sinking heart. "I have already given him permission to call upon me," she said, her voice unsteady.

"We must receive him if he calls, of course," Lady Hardwick said, a note of impatience coming into her voice, "but you are not to encourage him. Is that understood? I promised your parents that I would keep fortune hunters away, and I shall do so. If no other gentlemen have shown a distinguishing interest in you, it is your own fault for your provincial manners. I repeat, you are not to encourage Lord Courtney. Do you understand?"

"I understand," Letty replied, but an unaccustomed feeling of rebellion was rising in her breast. She *would* be forbidden to encourage the one gentleman who had shown her any kindness. Perhaps Lord Courtney did not have much money, but that did not necessarily mean that he liked her only because of hers.

Chapter Six

Lady Hardwick looked across the salon to where Sophie and Miss Alcock sat speaking to Mr. Eastman and Lord Lockwood, and smiled with satisfaction as she responded mechanically to the conversation of Mrs. Alcock. The Season was indeed now progressing well. Sophie had several admirers, and due to her judicious selection of Laetitia's wardrobe, her niece's presence had done little to detract from her daughter's. The only bad moments resulting from her niece's presence had been two occasions when she overheard some women commenting on the lack of guidance Miss Biddle must be receiving that she made so many social mistakes, but Society on the whole did not seem to hold her accountable for her niece's blunders. Indeed, many had privately sympathized with the task she had.

Of course, Lady Hardwick realized, much of this was to due Laetitia's fortune. Her money had indeed given them the entree to many places that had formerly been out of reach, beginning with the invitation to dinner at the Duchess of Grimwold's. In fact, Sophie had met one of her most eligible suitors, Lord Lockwood, at that dinner. Money was a great advantage, she thought, thinking of the carriage and the

91

new wardrobes she and her daughter had been able to acquire with the squire's money. She would miss the added income when Laetitia left. Perhaps she should purchase a few more items while her niece was still with her—she had heard that the classical mode was going to be replaced by the Egyptian, and would like her drawing room to be furnished in the first stare of fashion. Surely that would be a legitimate expense? One's house must be furnished elegantly in order to make the correct impression on one's callers.

"May we expect an announcement to be made soon?" Mrs. Alcock asked Lady Hardwick, following her hostess's gaze to Sophie and Lord Lockwood.

Lady Hardwick's thoughts left the furnishings and returned to her daughter. "It is too early to speculate," she replied, her expression giving Mrs. Alcock to understand that she might indeed expect an announcement in the near future.

The Alcocks took their departure soon afterward, followed by Mr. Eastman and Lord Lockwood. Sophie took a turn about the room, looking very pleased with herself.

"Mama, I do think I shall be receiving an offer soon," she confided to Lady Hardwick.

"From whom?" Lady Hardwick queried.

"Mr. Eastman—"

"Do not give him too much encouragement yet," Lady Hardwick cautioned. "Let us see if Lord Lockwood will come up to scratch. He would be a better match."

"Yes, Mama," Sophie agreed, "but I do not wish to depress Mr. Eastman's hopes unless he does." She left the room to instruct her maid to replace the blue ribands on one of her gowns with pink. Lord Lockwood had expressed his preference for that color.

Lady Hardwick remained in the salon, sorting

through their invitations and deciding which ones to accept.

"Lord Satre," the butler announced, interrupting her task.

Lord Satre entered the salon. He bent gracefully over Lady Hardwick's hand, kissing it lightly. "You are looking well, Lady Hardwick," he complimented her.

"Thank you, Lord Satre," Lady Hardwick replied. "Please sit down. Would you care for some refreshment? A glass of claret, perhaps?"

"No, thank you, Lady Hardwick. Is Miss Biddle not at home?" he asked, glancing about the salon. "I had hoped to speak with her."

"She has gone to call on Lady Wakeford this morning," Lady Hardwick explained.

"Lady Wakeford?" Lord Satre repeated. He appeared to hesitate a moment, and then seated himself in the chair next to Lady Hardwick. "I hope you will not consider me impertinent if I ask you if you think Lord Wakeford has an interest in your niece?"

Lady Hardwick looked at Lord Satre calculatingly. She had thought Lord Satre was intrigued with her niece only because of her ingenuousness; older rakes often were. Now it would appear he had a serious interest in Laetitia. "I do not believe so, Lord Satre. Rather, I suspect Lord Wakeford is quite put off by my niece's social blunders. He is the one who originally gave her the appellation 'Letty Loppet,' or so I have heard. I believe it is his sister who has an interest in Laetitia. She appears to have taken a liking to my niece."

"May I be frank with you, Lady Hardwick?" Lord Satre asked, looking at her penetratingly.

"Please."

"I find your niece a very attractive and charming

93

young girl, and indeed am becoming quite attached to her. However, I fear that my rank, or perhaps my age, might make her hesitate to look as high as myself. Perhaps you could smooth the way?"

Lady Hardwick hesitated. She knew her ability to influence her niece was limited, and besides, she had heard rumors about Lord Satre in his youth. She might not be overly fond of her niece, but she could not wish her any real harm.

"Perhaps you have heard I was rather wild in my youth," Lord Satre said, apparently reading her thoughts. "But I have settled down now, and wish to start a family. I could marry any woman I chose, but I find your niece's youth and freshness appealing. Her provincial manners and background do not revolt me. She needs an older man to guide her steps in Society."

He was silent a moment, and Lady Hardwick was silent, too, thinking furiously.

"Of course, I would make a generous settlement on your niece. Perhaps as her sponsor it would be appropriate for me to instruct my man of business to deposit the sum in your account until her financial arrangements are settled?"

Lady Hardwick looked at Lord Satre sharply, but his cold gray eyes did not give a clue to his thoughts. However, Lady Hardwick understood well enough. The money, once in her account, need never be transferred to Laetitia's. A short war with her conscience ensued. Lord Satre was considerably older than Laetitia — probably a full score and ten years. But her niece did need guidance in the ways of Society, and who better to provide it than a man of wealth, rank, and experience such as Lord Satre? Besides, she had promised her sister that she would not allow her to fall in the hands of a fortune hunter, and no one could accuse Lord Satre of being one. Yes, she could see that Lord Satre would indeed be the best choice for her niece.

"Lord Satre," she said finally, "you must understand that my influence with my niece is limited. However, as her sponsor for her come-out in Society, it is my duty to be sure she does not marry a fortune hunter, but makes a good match with a gentleman of rank and wealth. I should be failing in my duty otherwise," she ended virtuously.

"One could never accuse you of failing to see where your niece's best interests are, I am sure," he replied smoothly.

With another graceful bow Lord Satre left, leaving Lady Hardwick with an uncomfortable sensation of just having made a pact with the devil. She shook the feeling off impatiently. No one could say Lord Satre was not a good match for a squire's daughter whose fortune was tainted by trade.

Letty took another sip of the fragrant tea and placed the delicate Wedgwood cup on the table. She had been enjoying her call on the Wakefords very much. As Lady Wakeford had promised, Lord Wakeford was nowhere to be seen. Letty relaxed and talked happily with Lady Wakeford while the dowager countess looked on benignly, entering the conversation occasionally. Here was the kind of confidential conversation about fashions and the latest *on-dits* that Letty had dreamed of having with her cousin, a dream she now realized was not going to materialize.

Other callers at the Wakefords' came and went through the morning, but Letty felt so comfortable that she stayed on. She wished she could stay forever, she thought wistfully as she pictured the cold house to which she must return. When the time for nuncheon approached, she reluctantly rose to take her leave.

As she bade the dowager countess and Lady Wakeford good-bye, she heard footsteps coming up the stairs, and to her dismay, Lord Wakeford appeared at the door of the salon.

"Good morning, Miss Biddle," he said, "I hope Lady Hardwick and Miss Hardwick are well?"

"Yes, thank you, Lord Wakeford," Letty replied, wishing she had taken her departure five minutes earlier.

Lord Wakeford smiled charmingly and remembered his promise to his sister.

"I am glad I returned before you had taken your leave, Miss Biddle, as I wished to ask you if you would give me the pleasure of your company on a drive in the park this afternoon?"

Letty was reluctant to accept the invitation, but under the eyes of Lady Wakeford and the dowager countess could not refuse without appearing impolite.

"Thank you, Lord Wakeford, I should be pleased to go for a drive," she said, and escaped from the town house.

Letty and Daisy walked very slowly back to Lady Hardwick's, trying to prolong the good feelings of the morning. Daisy had been treated as well by the servants at the Wakefords as Letty had been by the countess and her daughter.

Inevitably, however, they reached Adam Street, and Letty joined her aunt and cousin in the Grand Salon. She could tell her aunt of the Wakefords' graciousness to her that morning. At least she had done one thing right.

"Where have you been all this time, miss?" Lady Hardwick demanded as Letty entered the salon.

Letty looked at her aunt in bewilderment as she sat down.

"Why, at the Wakefords'. You gave me permission to call on them this morning."

"You have been there all this time?"

"Yes."

"Three hours!" Lady Hardwick exclaimed in displeasure. "You must realize that the proper length for a morning call is fifteen minutes; thirty at the outmost if they are close friends. How mortifying. I suppose the dowager countess was there, too."

"In the country we stay that long and longer," Letty excused herself feebly. "I did not realize." She should have, she thought in despair as she remembered the short calls she had made mornings with her aunt, and how quickly the other callers had come and gone at the Wakefords' that morning.

"How often must I remind you that you are not in the country anymore? Longer calls are acceptable in the country because it takes longer to go somewhere. You are not in the country anymore, and I do not wish to hear any more about how things are done in Derbyshire. You are in *London*."

Letty's pleasure in her call to the Wakefords' vanished. Just when she most wanted to make a good impression, she had made another blunder. Worse, Lord Wakeford had witnessed it. She could feel her cheeks redden with the memory. And she had to go on a drive with him that afternoon. She wondered why he had asked her. She sensed her mistakes were a source of amusement to him, and she always seemed to make her worst ones in his presence. In fact, she would not be surprised if he were the one who had given her the sobriquet "Letty Loppet."

When Jules arrived at four in the afternoon to take

Letty for the drive, he was shown up to the Grand Salon, where he found Lady Hardwick and Miss Hardwick. Miss Biddle was nowhere in evidence.

Lady Hardwick welcomed Lord Wakeford effusively. She did not understand his attentions to her niece. He did not need her money, and Laetitia was much too provincial for his sophisticated taste. She rather thought she had been correct in what she had told Lord Satre—that it was Lady Wakeford who had encouraged her brother to take notice of Laetitia. Lady Wakeford appeared to have taken an unaccountable liking to her niece. Well, she would use the situation to promote Sophie. Lord Wakeford would be an even better catch than Lord Lockwood.

Jules was not closely acquainted with the Hardwicks and had no desire to be. Despite Lady Hardwick's undeniably good blood, he saw them as examples of pushy social climbers. He remembered his sister's thought that Lady Hardwick was sponsoring Miss Biddle in hopes that her fortune would gain them the entree to a higher level of Society. It was not going to gain them the entree to Jules Wakeford. When Lady Hardwick seemed inclined to have him stay and talk, he smiled charmingly and protested that while he should like to partake of some refreshment, he could not leave his horses standing and would she please send for Miss Biddle. Lady Hardwick reluctantly agreed to his request and sent a footman to summon her niece.

Miss Biddle came into the salon wearing a dress of beige with a matching pelisse. She looked neat and the clothes were modishly cut, but Jules wondered fleetingly why such a beautiful girl always wore such unflattering styles. He decided she must have an uneducated taste.

As he drove toward the park, Jules thought that

Miss Biddle seemed a different girl from the one he had seen at the ball the night before. She was quiet and subdued, and quite a contrast from the glowing girl he had observed dancing with Lord Courtney. He exerted himself to be amusing, but as they reached the park and her spirits had still not improved, Jules began to feel piqued. Here he was, putting himself out to take the chit for a drive and raise her credit, and far from appreciating his condescension, she seemed not to even wish to be in his company. He gave up trying to converse, and planned to return her to the Hardwicks' as soon as he could politely do so.

As Jules made his way toward the circular drive in Hyde Park, where all the fashionables paraded in the afternoon, he was surprised when Miss Biddle suddenly addressed him.

"It was you who gave me the nickname, was it not?"

Jules jerked the reins in surprise, and his cattle, not used to such treatment, grew skittish. Jules was shocked by Miss Biddle's question. It was not the thing for her to ask such a question, even if she did suspect him. It put him in an uncomfortable position, and one did not do that to one's escort.

When he had calmed his horse, he turned to look at her, and was disconcerted by the steady blue gaze he encountered. He looked away uncomfortably. Changing his mind about joining the crowds in the ring, he made for less-traveled roads in the park.

"Yes, Miss Biddle," he said after a lapse of several minutes, "it was I. I assure you, however, I did not intend that it become generally known. It was only something I said in jest to the Beau in passing conversation."

"I thought as much," she replied quietly. "I have known you found my provincial manners quite diverting, ever since the dinner at the duchess's."

"Please forgive me if I have inadvertently caused you pain or embarrassment by my words," Lord Wakeford said, hating her for putting him in a spot where he had to apologize, although he rather thought his sister would enjoy his discomfiture if she knew.

"It makes no difference, Lord Wakeford," Miss Biddle said almost indifferently. "Society already thought it of me. You only put it into words."

Lord Wakeford's discomfort increased. Evidently his sister had been correct. Miss Biddle's wealth did not shield her from all pain and hurt. This indifferent young woman was not the same one he had glimpsed at the ball the previous night. Jules's savoir faire deserted him and he turned his curricle homeward, not knowing what else to do.

He stopped in front of the Hardwicks' town house, and his groom, who had been waiting patiently, came forward to hold the horses while Jules helped Miss Biddle down from the curricle. As he walked with her to the door, Jules spoke impulsively.

"Miss Biddle, would you accompany me for a walk in St. James's Park tomorrow afternoon?" At least he had broken through her reserve, he thought as her eyes flew open wide at his unexpected invitation.

"Thank you, Lord Wakeford, but —" She stopped, looking down the street to where a black curricle was rounding the corner and proceeding in their direction. "Thank you, Lord Wakeford, I shall be pleased to accompany you," she said, obviously changing her mind.

"I shall call for you at four," he said, wondering why the sight of Lord Satre's curricle coming up the street had made her change her mind about accompanying him. Perhaps he was the lesser of two evils to the young girl, he thought ironically.

As Jules drove home, he wondered just what had possessed him to issue another invitation to Miss Biddle. She obviously had no desire for his company. Perhaps that was it. He was not accustomed to being dismissed so cavalierly by young girls. Or perhaps it was guilt over the truth of her accusations. Or both.

The next afternoon, as Letty walked beside Lord Wakeford through St. James's Park, she wondered why he seemed to be singling her out for attention. Yesterday the drive in Hyde Park, today a walk in St. James's Park. Perhaps, she thought, he felt guilty about labeling her "Letty Loppet." Or perhaps it was Lady Wakeford's influence. Whichever, it had saved her from a drive with Lord Satre. She had feared when she saw his curricle the previous afternoon that he might be calling to ask her for a drive, and so it had proved. She had seen that her aunt was not best pleased when she had begged a prior engagement, but she could not object.

If only it were Lord Courtney she was with, she thought wistfully. She had not seen him since the night of the ball, and she would not see him that night, either, since it was Wednesday and she would remain at home while her aunt and Sophie attended the assembly at Almack's. Perhaps she would see him the following night, at the opera.

"Miss Biddle," her escort's voice penetrated her thoughts. Letty started guiltily and looked at Lord Wakeford. "I am sorry, Lord Wakeford, I was wool-gathering," she apologized.

"I merely said we should be changing direction," he said, indicating another path. "I have a surprise for you."

Wondering what it could be, she followed his lead. Letty was enjoying St. James's Park even more than Hyde Park. It had beautiful beds of flowers, grass, trees, lakes — all that Hyde Park did — and was less crowded. She began to succumb to its beauty and relaxed, not even minding Lord Wakeford's company.

"Why, there are even cows here," she exclaimed suddenly, correctly identifying some shapes in the distance.

"Yes, that is my surprise," Lord Wakeford said. "Come," he commanded, leading her toward the faint figures. "Here in St. James's Park one can buy fresh milk and drink it on the spot," he explained. "I thought you would enjoy some."

"I see," Letty said, stopping and turning to face Lord Wakeford angrily, her previous enjoyment vanishing. "You decided that a rustic such as myself must long for milk directly from the cow," she accused him, hurt by what she felt was Lord Wakeford's intentionally poking fun at her.

Lord Wakeford's expression changed from one of merriment to one of chagrin, anger, and disappointment. "I assure you, I had intended no insult, Miss Biddle. An appreciation of fresh milk is not confined to persons from the country. Many Londoners come here for a pleasurable outing. If I was mistaken in thinking you would enjoy it, too, I beg your pardon."

Letty felt abashed. She was being far too thinskinned. Lord Wakeford had planned what he felt would be an enjoyable outing, and her behavior was downright churlish.

"Forgive me, Lord Wakeford," she said, placing her hand on his arm in entreaty. "I fear I am being oversensitive. I have, in fact, missed the fresh milk I used to drink in Derbyshire. I have found that by the time the milk is carried through the streets of London and arrived at my aunt's home, it often tastes as though it is on the verge of turning."

Lord Wakeford smiled his acceptance of her apology, and to her surprise took the hand she had placed on his arm and held it in his as he led her toward the cows. As she savored a cup of the frothy warm milk, Letty found that she was actually enjoying Lord Wakeford's company. He did not seem nearly so supercilious here. She smiled her appreciation at Lord Wakeford, unaware of the charming picture she presented with a snowy film of milk froth upon her lips. She instinctively licked it off, and Lord Wakeford looked at her with an odd expression.

After they drank their fill of the milk, they walked about the park, and Letty found she was almost in charity with Lord Wakeford by the time they arrived back at the Hardwicks' town house.

"I trust I shall see you at Almack's this evening," Lord Wakeford said as he accompanied her to the door.

Letty looked at him in surprise. "No. I do not have vouchers, although my aunt and cousin will be in attendance."

An angry look crossed Lord Wakeford's face, but he spoke kindly to Letty. "You are not missing a thing by not attending the assemblies at Almack's, Miss Biddle. I promise you they are very overrated. My sister rarely attends, and I may not myself."

"I shall be attending the opera tomorrow night," Letty surprised herself by offering.

"Then I shall see you there," Lord Wakeford said, bowing, and taking his leave as Letty entered the house.

As Lord Wakeford drove away, Letty wondered what had possessed her to volunteer that she would be at the opera. It was Lord Courtney she wished to see at the opera, not Lord Wakeford.

Letty prepared herself for her first appearance at the opera with great care. She dressed in one of the more attractive gowns Lady Hardwick had selected for her, a chemise dress of apricot muslin. While the color did little for her, the soft style was flattering to her slight figure, and her carnelians complemented the gown. Lady Hardwick sent her dresser to inspect Letty's toilette. After looking her over critically, the women left, to return shortly with two ostrich feathers and a bandeau for Letty's hair. Evidently Lady Hardwick wished her entire party, niece included, to look their best for their first appearance at the opera.

When they arrived at the Royal Opera House, Letty forgot all her problems in her awe at her surroundings. She stared at the opulently painted ceiling, illuminated by the immense chandeliers with their hundreds of candles, and admired the red, gold, and white decorated theater.

The Hardwicks had a box in the second tier at the right side. After Letty was seated, she spent her time admiring the other patrons until the opera began. The women were clad in glistening silks and satin, with magnificent jewels glittering at their throats and in their hair. The men were all in full evening dress, with silk breeches, stockings, and carrying folded *chapeau bras* under their arms. The pit below them was very noisy, with rowdy young bucks who openly ogled the women and occasionally shouted compliments or impolite comments.

When the performance of *The Magic Flute* finally began, Letty was totally captivated from the moment Tamino ran onstage pursued by a great serpent and was saved by three beautiful veiled ladies. *This* was what she had dreamed London would be like. She forgot all her disappointment in the Season, her troubles with her aunt and cousin, and even her nickname, and became lost in the opera until the first intermission brought her back down to earth. Stagehands began shifting the scenery around on the stage, and the patrons began to get up and move about, going to other boxes to visit with friends.

Lord Lockwood and Lord Satre were the first to arrive at the Hardwicks' box. Lord Lockwood devoted himself to Sophie, leaving Lord Satre to Lady Hardwick and Letty. Letty's delight with the evening began to dissipate as the uncomfortable feeling she always had around Lord Satre returned. However, it was only a few minutes before Lord Wakeford appeared at their box, and when Lord Courtney appeared soon afterward, Letty was in alt. Letty saw her aunt stiffen slightly at Lord Courtney's arrival, but she could not refuse to admit him. Lord Courtney gave Letty a conspiratorial look that seemed to say, I know what your aunt thinks of me, but see how she has to receive me anyway.

Somehow, the two younger gentlemen managed to sit with Letty, leaving Lord Satre with Lady Hardwick, and her uncomfortable feeling vanished. She began to feel quite relaxed, and her natural gaiety, which had been so little in evidence since she had come to London, returned.

"Are you finding your first visit to the opera enjoyable?" Lord Courtney inquired of her.

"Oh, I like it above all things," Letty enthused. "It is so exciting and colorful."

Lord Wakeford, who had been watching Miss Biddle's animated attitude with pleasure and surprise, smiled and teased her gently.

"It is not at all the thing to display such enthusiasm, for the performance, Miss Biddle. One is supposed to be more interested in the presence and attire of the other patrons than in the opera itself."

Letty was not sure whether Lord Wakeford was teasing or criticizing her, but found she did not care.

"Oh, I am interested in them, too," she said airily. "The women are so fine and wear so many jewels. Especially the ones in the center boxes," she finished, waving her fan in their general direction.

There was a sudden silence in the box at her words. Sophie looked startled, and Lady Hardwick hastily asked Lord Satre a question about one of the singers.

Lord Wakeford's face displayed the smile Letty had come to hate, and she knew she had made another mistake, although she had no idea what it could have been. She looked enquiringly at Lord Courtney.

Lord Courtney leaned toward her and spoke softly. "The women in the center boxes are of the *demimonde,* Miss Biddle. You are not supposed to be aware of their existence, much less speak of them or point them out. Ladies of rank sit in the side boxes, those of gentle birth but less wealth in the side galleries."

So that was it. Such a fuss over nothing, Letty thought. "I think it should be the other way around," she stated daringly. "They have the much better seats. It is difficult to see the stage properly from the side."

Jules thought to himself that the chit had a great deal of spirit, and smiled. He would repeat her reply as well as her comment when he recounted the story to the Beau. Jules noticed the workers had finished moving the props about on the stage. Knowing the second act would begin shortly, he took his leave from the Hardwicks. The others soon followed.

Letty became lost in the performance again, and when she slipped between the sheets of her bed that night, she reflected that the evening had been quite the most pleasant one she had spent since her arrival in London. Perhaps things were going to change for the better.

Chapter Seven

After the opera Letty realized that her attitude toward her aunt and cousin had undergone a substantial change. When she had first arrived in London, she had been happy to see her relatives, and had looked forward to being friends with Sophie. Soon, however, she had sensed that Sophie and her aunt did not truly like her, and a distance had manifested itself between them. The social errors she had made deepened the gulf. At first Letty had felt shame that her behavior had caused Sophie and Lady Hardwick embarrassment, and had tried her best to correct her mistakes and behave in a socially correct manner. But now she was beginning to feel a resentment toward them, no matter how she tried to stifle it. Letters from her mother and father had fueled this feeling, for Letty deduced from them that it was her father's money that was paying for most of the expenses for the Season — for her aunt and cousin as well as for herself.

Letty's realizations removed the burden of gratitude from her, and she was able to guess at her relatives' motives for their treatment of her with greater accuracy. She decided her earlier suspicion that she was being intentionally dressed in unflattering clothes was correct. She looked with dissatisfaction at her image in the glass. A new resolution came over her. She would not allow her aunt and cousin to ruin her Season. She could go to the modiste herself and order some more becoming clothes. She rang for Daisy, and they set out for Pall Mall.

Madame Parenteau recognized the young heiress and ushered her immediately into a private room. The modiste had guessed from the gossip of her other customers that it must be Miss Biddle's money that was paying her bills. Therefore, she did not hesitate to assist the young girl when Miss Biddle asked help in selecting flattering patterns and materials. If Lady Hardwick did not approve, that was not her worry.

Letty chose fuller styles and ordered several of the new tunic dresses in silks, two chemise dresses with full gathered tops, three new walking dresses, a curricle cloak of blue velvet, and a pelisse of pink lawn. On impulse, she also ordered two new riding habits. She had not been able to ride in town, but she would be glad for them when she returned to Derbyshire. She had decided she had ordered everything she needed, when she saw a beautiful red paduasoy among the materials the assistant had brought out.

"Perhaps the same material in a different color would be more suitable for a young girl just making her come-out," Madame Parenteau suggested tactfully, seeing her customer's liking for the material.

Letty was listening to the modiste with only half an ear. She was remembering a dress of this shade of red her mother had given her at Christmas one year, and how her father had called her his little red angel when she wore it. She fingered the heavy rich silk and held the material before her, seeing in the glass how the rich red brought a glow to her cheeks and enhanced the luster of her dark curls.

"No, I want this color," she insisted, "in a robe to be

109

worn over a gold embroidered petticoat, I think."

Madame Parenteau hesitated, wondering if she should try harder to steer the young woman away from a style and color that were definitely not suitable for a young girl. The mulish look that had crossed the girl's face at her first gentle objection decided the modiste to remain silent. Miss Biddle might cancel her entire order if she were angered. With a shrug she added the gown to the order. The other gowns the girl had selected were suitable, and surely when her aunt saw the red one she would prevent her niece from wearing it.

Letty left the shop feeling very pleased with herself. She had even thought to take the precaution of asking the gowns be delivered early in the morning before her aunt and cousin were awake. She envisioned herself appearing at a ball in one of the new gowns, and could hardly wait until they were ready. At last the Season was going to be what she had hoped for.

That Saturday the Hardwicks and Letty were invited to a breakfast at the Arlingtons'. Lady Arlington was trying to follow the style of the Duchess of Devonshire, who had started the custom of inviting guests large breakfasts.

Letty thought that "breakfast" was an odd name for a meal served at three o'clock, and conducted in a manner that was chaotic, to say the least. There were tables upon tables heavily laden with food and crammed with guests. However, there were not enough chairs for everyone present. Those who had arrived late stood about until they saw a place empty, and then tried to grab the chair before anyone else could.

Sophie had managed to seize a place next to Mr. Eastman by the simple expedient of shoving a rival aside, and Lady Hardwick had gotten a chair at the other end of the table. Letty was standing by the wall, thinking it was not worth trying to sit down and eat, when she heard a voice at her side.

"It is a sad crush, is it not, Miss Biddle?" Lord Wakeford commented.

"Yes. You may ridicule me on my country ways, but we do not serve breakfast at three in the afternoon, nor force our guests to fight for a place to sit at our tables," Letty replied, smiling at seeing a familiar face.

"I see you are never going to forgive my being responsible for your nickname," Lord Wakeford said ruefully.

"I may consider it," Letty replied archly. It was difficult to remain on the outs with such a handsome gentleman. Besides, she was very fond of his sister.

"I see I shall have to earn your forgiveness," Lord Wakeford said. "Perhaps by obtaining you a seat?" he asked, possessing himself of a chair as a guest finished his repast and rose to leave.

"Thank you," Letty said, taking the chair he offered and smiling at him gratefully.

"Would you walk with me in Kensington Gardens tomorrow?" Lord Wakeford asked as he finished seating Letty. "I can promise it will be a peaceful contrast to this crush."

"Thank you, I should enjoy that," Letty replied. Lord Wakeford smiled his pleasure and then left her with a quick bow as he saw another place empty farther down the table.

Letty looked after Lord Wakeford. He could be quite charming when he chose. She supposed she had been too unforgiving. Thoughtfully, she turned her attention to the food and helped herself to some meat pie and fruit.

"Would you pass me some of that delicious-looking ham?" she heard a familiar voice say, and turned to her

111

right, delighted to see that Lord Courtney was taking the chair next to hers. "Lord Courtney," she said, a pleased smile on her face.

"Good afternoon, Miss Biddle. The gods are smiling on me today, to cause Mr. Alcock to leave the chair next to yours just as I arrived. Even better, your aunt is nowhere near."

Letty laughed. "It is true Aunt Henrietta does not approve of you. She told me you are a fortune hunter."

Lord Courtney did not join in her laughter, but looked at Letty intently. "It is true I do not have much money, Miss Biddle," he said quietly, "but I give you my word that your money is not what captured my interest. Were I only seeking wealth, there are many women whom it would be easier to attract, women whose fortunes are not controlled by their fathers until they are of age."

Letty brightened at Lord Courtney's last comment. That was true. Lord Courtney could not possibly be after her fortune if he knew her father would control it for three years yet.

"I suppose Lady Hardwick suspects most of your suitors of being fortune hunters," Lord Courtney commented, taking some strawberries and offering them to Letty.

"Not quite all. She has told me that Lord Satre does not need money, and I do not think she suspects Lord Wakeford of being a fortune hunter."

"Lord Wakeford is one of your suitors?" Lord Courtney asked, a note of surprise in his voice.

"I suppose I should not call him a suitor, precisely," Letty acknowledged, "but he has been seeking my company quite often. It has rather puzzled me, to be honest."

Lord Courtney laid down his fork and looked at Letty hesitantly. "I am not sure I should repeat gossip

112

MORE PASSION AND ADVENTURE AWAIT... YOUR TRIP TO A BIG ADVENTUROUS WORLD BEGINS WHEN YOU ACCEPT YOUR FIRST 4 NOVELS ABSOLUTELY *FREE*
(AN $18.00 VALUE)

Accept your Free gift and start to experience more of the passion and adventure you like in a historical romance novel. Each Zebra novel is filled with proud men, spirited women and tempestuous love that you'll remember long after you turn the last page.

Zebra Historical Romances are the finest novels of their kind. They are written by authors who really know how to weave tales of romance and adventure in the historical settings you love. You'll feel like you've actually gone back in time with the thrilling stories that each Zebra novel offers.

GET YOUR FREE GIFT WITH THE START OF YOUR HOME SUBSCRIPTION

Our readers tell us that these books sell out very fast in book stores and often they miss the newest titles. So Zebra has made arrangements for you to receive the four newest novels published each month.

You'll be guaranteed that you'll never miss a title, and home delivery is so convenient. And to show you just how easy it is to get Zebra Historical Romances, we'll send you your first 4 books absolutely FREE! Our gift to you just for trying our home subscription service.

BIG SAVINGS AND FREE HOME DELIVERY

Each month, you'll receive the four newest titles as soon as they are published. You'll probably receive them even before the bookstores do. What's more, you may preview these exciting novels free for 10 days. If you like them as much as we think you will, just pay the low preferred subscriber's price of just $3.75 each. *You'll save $3.00 each month off the publisher's price.* AND, your savings are even greater because there are never any shipping, handling or other hidden charges—FREE Home Delivery. Of course you can return any shipment within 10 days for full credit, no questions asked. There is no minimum number of books you must buy.

GET
FOUR
FREE
BOOKS
(AN $18.00 VALUE)

ZEBRA HOME SUBSCRIPTION
SERVICE, INC.
P.O. Box 5214
120 BRIGHTON ROAD
CLIFTON, NEW JERSEY 07015-5214

to you, Miss Biddle, but it distresses me that you may be unknowingly fueling the jokes about your provincial ways."

"Whatever do you mean, Lord Courtney?" Letty asked, looking at him curiously.

Lord Courtney turned away as though regretting he had said anything, and then looked back to her with an air of resolution. "I must tell you, even if it should prove distressing. Miss Biddle, it is generally known that Lord Wakeford has been entertaining the Beau and other frequenters of White's with tales of your social blunders. It has made him quite popular with Beau Brummell."

Lord Courtney correctly surmised that Letty would not know that Lord Wakeford had long been an intimate of the Beau, nor that she was far from being the only young woman so honored. He watched Letty's reaction to his words closely.

Letty felt a great rage come over her as she listened to Lord Courtney. So *that* was why Lord Wakeford had been seeking her company! It was despicable! She looked down at her plate, trying to bring her emotions under control.

"I am sorry, Miss Biddle, I seem to have overset you," Lord Courtney said concernedly as he saw the color of her cheeks fluctuate between the red of anger and the white of mortification.

Letty turned back to Lord Courtney, and made an effort to smile as he looked at her with an expression of kind concern. "I am not overset, Lord Courtney. I already suspected something of the sort, you have only confirmed those suspicions. Please let us talk of more agreeable matters."

Letty resolutely banished the perfidious Lord Wakeford from her mind. She flirted shamelessly with Lord Courtney, reveling in the fact that one gentleman, at least, found her company pleasing for reasons other than selfish amusement.

Jules prepared to collect Miss Biddle for their walk in Kensington Gardens with a feeling of anticipation. He was actually beginning to enjoy the chit's company. It was as his sister had told him from the beginning — Miss Biddle was a charming, unaffected girl, very unlike the usual affected Society misses.

But to his surprise, when he picked her up she seemed a very different person from the girl of yesterday. He thought perhaps she was simply tired, and tried to entertain her with amusing stories during the drive to the Gardens, but she failed to respond. Perhaps the beauty of the Gardens would dispel her odd mood. The flowers outside the Palace were exceptionally fine this year. The atmosphere of the Gardens was always peaceful, for no riding was allowed. The Gardens were open to pedestrians on Sundays, and then only to the gentry.

Jules left his curricle with his groom and escorted Miss Biddle into the Gardens, sure her spirits would lighten. However, she kept her attention strictly on the flowers, and all his efforts could not shake her from her megrims. At last he gave up and escorted her directly back to the Hardwicks' instead of stopping by his home to call on his mother and sister as he had planned. As the door closed behind her, he shook his head in puzzlement. What could possibly have happened to change her so drastically since the previous afternoon?

Later that week Letty's parcels began to arrive from the modiste's. Letty's spirits, which had been quite cast down over Lord Courtney's revelations about Lord Wakeford, rose again in her excitement over her new gowns. She and Daisy unwrapped the parcels eagerly, and Letty tried several of the gowns on. As she viewed her reflection in the glass, Letty knew that she had been correct in her suspicions that her aunt had chosen clothes for her that were unflattering. *These* gowns enhanced her looks.

"Oh, miss! You look beautiful," Daisy breathed.

Letty smiled and thanked her maid for the compliment, immodestly agreeing with her assessment.

"I think I shall wear the red gown to the ball tonight," she said, thinking of Lord Courtney and wishing to look her best. A thought of Lord Wakeford also came into her mind. He could not accuse her of looking like a rustic in this gown. She would like to see a look of admiration in his eyes instead of the amused smile he seemed to reserve for her alone.

That evening, as she stood ready to go, Letty thought the gown everything she had hoped it would be. The deep red made her skin glow and her hair shine. Her garnets, too, looked well with the deep red. Her only worry was what her aunt would say when she saw the gown. She was trying to decide what to say to Lady Hardwick, when her cousin walked unannounced into her room.

"I want to look at your ribands—" She broke off as she noticed Letty's gown.

"*Where* did you get that dress?" Sophie demanded, shocked.

"I ordered some gowns myself when I was out with Daisy one morning," Letty said defiantly.

Sophie, attractive in her favorite light blue, looked at her cousin again, and her expression of shock and anger was replaced by one of cunning.

115

"Mama will not like you wearing a gown she did not select," Sophie said after a pause. "Cover it completely with your cloak before you go downstairs. When we arrive at the Palmers' you had best pretend to have some difficulty with your toilette and go to the retiring room. That way I can get Mama to go into the ballroom before she sees your gown, and she will not be able to send you home to change," she advised, and, forgetting the ribands, left Letty's room.

Sophie's willingness to help her gave Letty pause, for it was quite out of character. She looked again at her reflection in the glass, wondering if there was something wrong with her appearance but was reassured by her image. Her desire to appear in public looking as well as she could overcame her caution. Daisy helped her adjust her full evening cloak so not a trace of red showed, and she waited to join her aunt in the hall until the last minute so Lady Hardwick would be impatient to leave and not ask to see what her niece was wearing.

In the entrance hall of the Palmers' town house, Letty followed her cousin's advice and pretended to have trouble with the fastenings of her cloak, and as she removed the hood, she exclaimed that her hair was coming loose. She urged her aunt and Sophie to go ahead to the ballroom, and Sophie seconded her, saying that Letty could go find a maid to help her repair her coiffure and join them in the ballroom later.

As soon as Lady Hardwick and Sophie were out of sight, Letty asked a footman the way to the retiring room, and went to a wait there until she felt sure the ball was under way and it was safe to join her aunt.

Jules stood at the side of the ballroom with casual grace, speaking to Beau Brummell and watching the arriving guests. He realized with surprise that he was watching for Miss Biddle. The chit seemed to be occupying his thoughts to a great extent, he mused. He saw Lady Hardwick and her daughter enter the ballroom, but Miss Biddle was not with them. When Lord and Lady Palmer left their places by the door and began to mingle with the other guests, Letty had still not arrived. Perhaps she was feeling indisposed and had not come.

"Where is the Biddle heiress?" Beau Brummell asked, interrupting Jules's thoughts. "You have not had any amusing stories about her with which to regale us recently." The Beau flicked his jeweled snuff box open with his thumb and dipped his index finger into the powder with matchless grace. His court watched his actions closely, most planning to practice before their mirrors the Beau's manner of taking snuff.

"She has not made many social gaffes lately," Jules said, taking his attention from the doorway and turning to the Beau. " 'Letty Loppet' is no longer apropos."

Even as he finished speaking, there was a collective gasp and a momentary hush. All eyes seemed to be on the doorway he had been watching, and Jules turned back curiously. There, framed in the gilt entrance, was Miss Biddle. She was scanning the guests, evidently searching for her aunt and cousin.

"I do not think we need rename her quite yet," the Beau said, smiling.

Jules felt a sick dismay as he took in Miss Biddle's attire, and heard comments about it begin to circulate. The red gown became her magnificently, and would have been most appropriate if she were not a young girl. Did she not know that girls making their comeouts did not wear red? She looked like a member of the *demi-monde,* albeit a wealthy and beautiful one. He

117

felt a surge of anger at her aunt for allowing Miss Biddle to wear such a gown, and glanced at Lady Hardwick, realizing immediately from her expression that she was as shocked as the rest of the company. He looked back at Miss Biddle and could see that her color was slowly mounting as she became aware she was the cynosure of all eyes.

The Beau made a droll comment, but Jules did not reply. He was too concerned for Miss Biddle. Even her wealth would not protect her if she appeared too fast. He wondered if anyone would dare dance with her, and decided to offer himself as a partner. He was aware that as he was an intimate of the Beau, Society would follow his lead. If he danced with her, so would others. It might minimize the damage she had done her reputation by wearing the dress. He walked purposefully across the floor.

"Lady Hardwick, good evening," he said, addressing himself first to Miss Biddle's angry-looking aunt. "I have come to ask if I might have the honor of partnering your niece for the boulanger."

"It is good of you, I am sure, Lord Wakeford," Lady Hardwick said with a thin smile. "Letty," she prodded, fixing her niece with a basilisk stare.

"Thank you, Lord Wakeford, I should be delighted," Letty said, speaking the prescribed words in a flat voice.

Jules held out his hand, and Letty rose. Her high color and stiff manner showed Jules she was aware of the solecism she had committed in wearing the dress, but she held her head high, and he admired her spirit. It must be an extremely humiliating situation for a young girl inexperienced in Society. The chit had pluck.

"Smile," he commanded her in a low voice as they took their places on the floor.

118

Miss Biddle obediently stretched her lips in the semblance of a smile. If Jules could see its hollowness, he knew it would not be discernible from a distance. He smiled in turn, to make it evident to all watching, that he, Lord Wakeford, Marquess of Thornhill, found Miss Biddle's company both agreeable and entertaining.

Jules kept his eyes on Letty when the movements of the dance brought them together, but when they were apart he carefully observed the reaction of the other guests to his partner. He was pleased to note that she was no longer receiving the contemptuous regard she had been upon her entrance into the ballroom. His plan was working. By the time he returned Letty to her aunt at the conclusion of the dance, he had no doubt that his attention to her had had the desired effect, and that other gentlemen would also ask her to dance.

As Jules walked away from the Hardwicks, it occurred to him that there was something else he could do to help Miss Biddle. The Duchess of Grimwold was at the ball, and a word in her ear might persuade her to help Letty by proclaiming her an original. After all, the duchess was an original herself. He remembered her teasing Letty about the neat's tongue, and knew the old lady had a liking for the girl.

Although it had only begun, the evening seemed interminable to Letty. Her aunt had been furious at her for the dress. Surely Sophie must have known. Looking at the gleeful expression on her cousin's face, Letty knew she should have listened to the voice that had urged caution at Sophie's unusual willingness to help her. Letty wondered sadly what she had ever done to make her cousin dislike her so.

She turned away from Sophie and her aunt, unable

119

to decide whether it was better to sit silently by her angry aunt or to dance with gentlemen she was sure were secretly laughing at her or thinking she was fast. Like Lord Wakeford. Remembering what Lord Courtney had told her at the breakfast, she had not wanted to dance with the marquess. No doubt Lord Wakeford, diverted by her disgrace, had been hoping for material for new stories to tell the Beau. Although, she recalled, Lord Wakeford's smile had appeared almost genuine, and his eyes had expressed understanding. At least he had been better than her second partner. Lord Satre had leered at her more than ever, his insinuating glances making her feel the harlot her aunt had told her she appeared in her new dress.

"Miss Biddle"—a voice interrupted her thoughts—"if you do not have a partner for this next dance, may I have the honor?"

"Thank you, Lord Courtney," Letty said, a smile of pleasure and gratitude transforming her face.

"I wish I had seen you before you entered the ballroom, Miss Biddle," the viscount said as they walked onto the floor. "I would have warned you and you could have returned home to put on a different gown."

"I think I shall never understand all the rules," Letty replied despairingly. "My aunt tells me the gown would have been acceptable were I married."

"That is true," Lord Courtney corroborated as they took their places in the set. "Married women are not bound by many of the rules you find so trying," he said, looking at her meaningfully.

Letty felt her breath quicken at his words, and she covered her confusion by changing the direction of the subject. "It seems to me it must be easier for the gentlemen than the women in Society, Lord Courtney. You do not have so many rules."

Lord Courtney followed her conversational lead. "I

suppose it is true you have more rules, but we gentle-men have rules, too. For instance, a gentleman may not ask a younger sister to dance unless an older one already has a partner. And we must be sure that we dance with the daughter of our host at least once of an evening, no matter how fubsy-faced she may be."

Letty smiled gratefully, appreciating Lord Courtney's efforts to put her at ease. When the dance was over, he asked her if she would like to get a breath of fresh air and escape the eyes of the company a mo-ment. Letty thankfully agreed. It would feel good to get out of the heat of the ballroom. He escorted her from the room, and she went to the edge of the bal-cony, lifting her face to the breeze. A touch on her shoulder made her turn. Lord Courtney stood close behind her. He took her hands in his, and Letty felt herself blush.

"Miss Biddle," he said, "I know I should not speak to you before I have spoken to your parents, but I must. I think you are not unaware of the feelings I have for you. Would you do me the honor of becoming my wife?"

Letty blushed and looked down in confusion. She was not surprised at his words, but she *was* surprised to find that she felt a faint doubt.

"Miss Biddle?" he asked. Letty looked up at him—he was so handsome and was the only one who had been unfailingly kind to her in London. How could she hesitate to accept his offer? It was of a moment like this she had long dreamed.

"Thank you, Lord Courtney," she replied. "It would be an honor."

He lifted her hand to his lips, and then, clasping it between his hands, began to draw her toward him, when their tête-à-tête was interrupted by the arrival of another couple seeking fresh air. He stepped back from her with a smile.

"I think it is best you not tell your aunt of what has passed between us quite yet," he advised softly.

"No, I should like to tell my parents first. I shall write them tomorrow."

A shade passed over Lord Courtney's face. "I think it would be better, Miss Biddle, if you were not to tell your parents yet, either. I should prefer to inform them myself."

"Of course, if that is what you wish," Letty agreed as he escorted her back into the ballroom.

Letty went through the rest of the evening in a state of euphoria. Not even the scold she knew she would receive from her aunt after they returned home made her unhappy, so secure she felt in Lord Courtney's love.

When they returned to the town house, Lady Hardwick ordered Letty into the small salon, and closed the door after her, shutting Sophie out.

"You will wear no more clothes that I have not selected," Lady Hardwick proclaimed. "You see what comes of attempting to select your own gowns. You have no idea what is suitable."

"Yes, Aunt," Letty agreed. Her aunt's words did not distress her in the slightest; indeed, she was hardly listening to Lady Hardwick, remembering Lord Courtney's words to her that evening.

"And you are not to see Lord Courtney again. I saw you go out onto the balcony in his company. I told you before, he is a fortune hunter. Lord Satre is a much more acceptable suitor."

These words of her aunt's captured Letty's attention. "Lord Satre? He must be over two score years my senior," she protested. "Besides, I do not like him. He makes me feel uncomfortable."

"You should be thankful to Lord Satre for saving you from disgrace this evening when you appeared in that red gown," Lady Hardwick said, looking at her niece in disapprobation. "It was his dancing with you that saved your reputation."

"He was not the only one who danced with me," Letty contradicted. "So did Lord Wakeford, Lord Arlington, Mr. Alcock, and many others. I did not sit out a single dance."

"They danced with you because Lord Satre asked you for his first one," Lady Hardwick said insistently. "I am seriously displeased with you. I had thought you were making more of an effort this past week, but the events of tonight show me I was wrong. You are quite unrepentant. I *forbid* you to see Lord Courtney. If he calls here, he shall be told you are indisposed, and if you meet him at entertainments, you are not to speak to him except in my presence. I shall ask Sophie to help me to be sure you obey my instructions. Now, go to your room and think upon your disgraceful behavior."

Letty's heart sank as she went slowly from the room, her aunt's angry gaze upon her back. What would she do now? Lord Courtney would think she had changed her mind and did not wish to marry him if her aunt carried out her threats. Whatever could she do?

Chapter Eight

Lady Hardwick did carry through her threat to instruct that Lord Courtney be told Letty was indisposed should he call. Letty sat in the Grand Salon the next morning feeling very put upon. Sophie looked especially smug and superior when her two favorite suitors, Lord Lockwood and Mr. Eastman, were announced. The attentions of both had been very marked, and Letty supposed it would not be long before her cousin received an offer.

Letty looked away from her cousin and her guests, pretending to be absorbed in her fancywork. She needed time to concentrate on the problem created by Lady Hardwick's refusing to allow her to see Lord Courtney. How was she going to get word to Lord Courtney that she was forbidden to see him? She had no idea how to go about sending him word without Lady Hardwick hearing of it.

A few moments later, hope came from an unexpected source. A servant entered the salon with a note for Letty from Lady Wakeford, who, remembering that Lady Hardwick left Letty home Wednesday nights while she and her daughter attended Almack's, invited Letty to join her at the opera that night. Perhaps Lord Courtney would be present at the opera,

Letty hoped as she asked permission from Lady Hardwick to go. She thought about sending a note to him, but she did not have his address and was not sure Daisy could find out without alerting Lady Hardwick's servants.

To Letty's delight, Lord Courtney did attend the opera that evening. He spotted Letty sitting with the Wakeford's and came to their box during the first intermission.

"I am glad to see you are feeling better, Miss Biddle," Lord Courtney said after he had paid his respects to the countess and Lady Wakeford. "I called upon you this morning, but was told you were indisposed."

Seeing that the dowager and Lady Wakeford were involved in conversation with another visitor to their box, Letty dared to tell Lord Courtney why he had been refused her company.

"My aunt has forbidden me to see you and has given instructions that you are to be told I am indisposed when you call," she explained in a low voice. "I have been quite overset, not knowing how to get word to you."

"Do not despair," Lord Courtney comforted Letty. "I shall still be able to see you at any entertainments to which we are both invited. Your aunt cannot forbid you to be civil to me in public." He pressed her hand reassuringly, and then, noting that they were attracting Lady Wakeford's attention, began to discuss the opera.

Lady Wakeford watched her young friend conversing with Lord Courtney with concern. She had feared Miss Biddle might be developing a *tendre* for Lord Courtney, and their intimate conversation seemed to bear out her suspicions. Her fears about such an unsuitable attachment overcame her natural reluctance to interfere, and after Lord Courtney departed she tried to warn her friend.

"I notice that Lord Courtney often seeks your company, Miss Biddle," she ventured to say.

"Yes, he has been most attentive," Letty confessed, wishing she could confide the whole. "But Aunt Henrietta has forbidden me to receive him at home. I do not know what to do."

"Is it wise to defy your aunt's wishes?" Lady Wakeford asked carefully. "She may have reasons for her action."

"What reasons?" Letty asked, feeling piqued that her only friend seemed to be taking the part of her aunt. "Lord Courtney is the only gentleman who has been truly kind to me here in London." At Lady Wakeford's questioning look, she attempted to explain more fully. "Oh, there are others who have been kind to me, too, at least outwardly, but I always feel they are laughing behind my back at my provincial manners. I never feel that with Lord Courtney."

Lady Wakeford knew she would have to tread carefully, but her genuine affection for the girl moved her to try.

"Miss Biddle, Lord Courtney may have his own reasons for appearing kind."

"You mean that he is poor," Letty said defensively, remembering to keep her voice low less the dowager overhear. "I know, for he has told me of his situation. That does not make him a fortune hunter. Why is it," she continued, a note of frustration entering her voice, "that everyone supposes any gentleman who shows me attention is interested only in my wealth? Is it not possible that someone might like me for myself, even should he chance to be poor?"

"Of course it is," Lady Wakeford reassured Letty. "But sometimes it may be difficult to distinguish between the two. If a gentleman who wishes to pay you court already has money, one knows that one's fortune is not the attraction."

"Perhaps such a gentleman simply desires more," Letty said cynically. "I suppose you would have me encourage Lord Satre. That is what my aunt wishes me to do."

"No. I do not think Lord Satre would be a good choice for you. But there are many other gentlemen of wealth and breeding closer to you in age."

"Such as your brother, I suppose, who gave me the name 'Letty Loppet.' "

At Lady Wakeford's stricken look, Letty felt contrite. "I am sorry, Lady Wakeford. Please forgive me," she begged.

Lady Wakeford smiled to show no offense was taken. "It is true Jules did give you the nickname. I cannot defend him, for it was wrong. I do know, though, that he did not mean to cause you pain. They were the thoughtless words of a moment, for which he is truly sorry."

"Perhaps," Letty said, "but the name stuck nevertheless."

Lady Wakeford saw tears glistening in Letty's eyes and placed her hand over the younger girl's, feeling compassion for her unhappiness. "I am sorry if my words have upset you. It is just that I am concerned for you and do not wish you to make a mistake in something as important as your marriage."

"I understand," Letty said, willing the tears away. "But you need not worry about Lord Courtney's motives. He is not what you fear, I am sure."

Lady Wakeford was not so sanguine, but knew she had done all she could to warn her friend and said no more.

After Lady Wakeford and her mother returned Letty home that evening, Lady Wakeford resolved to question her brother about Lord Courtney. Miss Biddle's interest in the undeniably charming viscount gave her serious feelings of disquiet. Perhaps Jules would know something about Lord Courtney that would ease her mind. She bade her mother good night and went directly upstairs. A light from under Jules's study door told her he was still awake, and she tapped lightly.

"Enter," Jules called, and Emily let herself in. Jules was seated behind his desk, absorbed in his accounts. She took a chair before the desk.

"Jules, what do you know of Lord Courtney?"

"Lord Courtney?" Jules asked, looking up from his work.

"Yes, I am worried about Miss Biddle's increasing interest in him."

"Miss Biddle's affections are none of our concern," Jules replied rather shortly, looking back down. It still rankled that after he had decided to condescend to take an interest in the Biddle chit and atone for giving her the nickname, she had continually refused to accept his overtures.

"I think it *is* our concern," Emily contradicted him. "It was the nickname you gave her and the stories you spread about her provincial manners that robbed her of her self-esteem and made her easy prey to an unscrupulous fortune hunter like Lord Courtney."

Jules pushed his accounts aside and stood, going to lean against the fireplace mantel. He stared into the flames thoughtfully. There was more truth in his sister's words than he cared to admit.

"The attachment has disturbed me, too," he confessed. "Not because Courtney is in need of funds, many are. He is a bad sort, though, ruthless. The duns are after him, and I suspect he is getting desperate for money."

"I wish I could think of some way to show Miss Biddle the truth about him," Emily said. "She will not listen to words. I fear Lady Hardwick is making matters worse by pressing her to accept Lord Satre as a suitor."

"Satre?" Jules asked in surprise. "That lecher? He is no better than Courtney. Worse, in fact. He is not in need of funds, but he has no morals whatsoever. I would not care to see any young woman in his hands. There are rumors he was involved in the Hell-fire Club in his youth."

Her brother's words increased Emily's distress. She was not completely sure what members of the Hell-fire Club had done, for such things were not discussed in the presence of an unmarried lady, but she knew that some of the most notorious rakes in the country had been involved in the club.

"Why not try to win Miss Biddle's affections yourself?" she suggested daringly.

"That's a crack-brained notion if I ever heard one," Jules scoffed, unwilling to admit to his sister that he had already made overtures of friendship to Miss Biddle and they had been firmly rejected. "Surely you would not wish me to hurt Miss Biddle by persuading her to care for me and then failing to offer for her."

"I do not think it would come to that," Emily said thoughtfully. "If you could just show her that a young gentleman of breeding and wealth could find her attractive . . ."

"That horse won't go," Jules replied, surprised to find the idea of Miss Biddle caring for him was not an unappealing one. "I admit the logic of the plan, but I am not the one to carry it out. She would never forgive the one who first called her 'Letty Loppet.' "

"I suppose you are correct," Emily admitted, remembering Miss Biddle's words earlier that evening, "but I do dislike seeing her in the clutches of Lord Courtney or Lord Satre."

Jules smiled at his sister's dramatization of the situation. "I promise to think on the problem, but I doubt there is anything we can do. Perhaps she will come to see Lord Courtney for what he is on her own," he finished with an encouraging smile.

"I hope so," Emily said doubtfully, rising. She gave her brother an affectionate kiss and left the study feeling little better about her friend than before.

After his sister left, Jules dropped into the chair she had vacated and frowned at the ceiling. The idea of Miss Biddle with Lord Courtney or Lord Satre troubled him more than it should. After all, she was nothing to him, just a chit from the country to whom his younger sister had happened to take a liking. No doubt he was feeling guilty about giving her the nickname, and did not want to feel she was being driven to an unsuitable match because of it. Yes, that must be why the thought was so disturbing.

Thursday morning Letty entered the Grand Salon to find her cousin in a state of suppressed excitement. Sophie's eyes sparkled, and she had a satisfied, almost glowing look. She smiled at Letty, and motioned her cousin to be seated next to her. Wondering why Sophie was being so friendly, Letty complied.

"Lord Lockwood is with Mama," Sophie said importantly. "He is asking permission to offer for me. He indicated to me last night at Almack's that he was going to call on Mama this morning."

"I thought you preferred Mr. Eastman," Letty let slip in her surprise.

"Oh, that boy," Sophie said dismissively. "He is only the Honorable *Mr.* Eastman. I shall be a countess when I marry Lord Lockwood."

"But Mr. Eastman is the son of an earl," Letty protested.

"Only a younger son and not likely to accede to the title. I would only be plain Mrs. Eastman."

Letty thought of the florid and rotund Lord Lockwood, fully a score of years older than Sophie, and mentally compared him to the youthful, charming Mr. Eastman. However, it was her cousin's choice to make, not hers, and she silenced her tongue.

Sophie, disappointed that her announcement had not had the effect on Letty she felt it should, tossed her head and moved to another chair. She waited there in silence until her mother came to tell her that Lord Lockwood was waiting to speak with her in the Small Salon. With a last triumphant look at her cousin, Sophie went to join her suitor.

"Now I must marry you off, and my duty will be done," Lady Hardwick said to Letty with satisfaction as she sat down in her favorite armchair.

"I am not sure I wish to marry," Letty replied, thinking that if she could not marry Lord Courtney, she would rather remain a spinster.

"Of course you do," Lady Hardwick said heartily in great good humor now that Sophie was to marry a lord. "Every young girl does. Why else did you wish to come to London and have a Season? Your mother wrote that it was to find a husband since there were no eligible gentlemen in Derbyshire."

Letty was silenced by this truth. She remembered her fear that she might never meet any suitors other than Tom Goodman. She had been no better than Sophie in her snobbishness, Letty saw with sudden insight. It seemed years ago, not weeks.

"I have changed my mind, Aunt," she said aloud. "I no longer feel that I must make a match this Season."

"Fustian," Lady Hardwick replied, an edge of impatience entering her voice. "I have reason to believe you will be receiving an excellent offer very soon."

Letty was dismayed. "If you refer to Lord Satre, I do not wish to marry him. Please do not give him permission to make me an offer if he approaches you."

"I most certainly will, and if you know what is good for you, you will accept," Lady Hardwick snapped, her good humor completely dissipating. "I have already written to your mother and father to inform them of Lord Satre's interest and advising that his suit be accepted."

Letty listened to her aunt's words with growing horror. Surely her parents would not listen to her aunt and insist that she accept Lord Satre? Lady Hardwick could not *force* her to marry Lord Satre if she did not wish to, could she?

She began to protest more strenuously, but was forced to abandon her arguments as Sophie, her face beaming, reentered the salon in the company of Lord Lockwood. Lady Hardwick forgot her recalcitrant niece in the ensuing congratulations, but Letty, although she tried to enter into the spirit of the occasion, had poor success. Sophie concluded her cousin's poor humor was caused by jealousy, and the thought added to the triumph of her day.

Letty's fears about Lord Satre were allayed over the next week. Lady Hardwick did not bring up the subject again, being immersed in making plans for her daughter's wedding, which was to take place in July.

Letty almost began to feel comfortable. She made no serious social errors, and was able to converse with Lord Courtney at several entertainments without her aunt or cousin noticing. She did wonder a little at herself for her unrepentant defiance of her aunt's wishes. A letter she received from Derbyshire caused her a twinge of guilt. Her parents would not approve her behavior. Lady Hardwick stood in their place while Letty lived in London, and she owed her obedience.

Her parents, however, did not know the whole story, Letty thought by way of an excuse. They would understand if they knew what Lord Satre was like. They had not mentioned him in their letter, and she supposed they had not yet received the letter from Lady Hardwick when they had written. How she would like to tell her parents the whole! She determined to ask Lord Courtney's permission to tell her parents of the betrothal the next time she saw him.

Letty had her chance to ask Lord Courtney at a ball that very night. When he approached her for a dance she asked if they might sit it out, as she had something important to ask him.

"Of course, Miss Biddle," he agreed, leading her to some chairs isolated from the others by large Doric columns and potted plants.

"Lord Courtney," Letty began.

"Stephen," he corrected her.

"Stephen," she began again, blushing. "I think we should tell my parents of our betrothal. You judge them by my aunt, but they are nothing alike. I am sure my parents would allow me to marry you when they see how necessary it is to my happiness."

"I know you wish to share the news with your parents," he said, "but we agreed to wait until after you return home at the end of the Season. If you tell them now, your aunt will oppose the match and present me in a bad light to your parents. Besides, I should like to be the one to speak to your father first," he said, a tender expression on his face.

Letty reluctantly agreed. "If you think it best. It is only that I dislike keeping my parents in the dark."

"It will not be for long," Lord Courtney assured her.

"The Season will be over in a month. Now," he said, "we had best rejoin the rest of the company before your aunt wonders where you have gone."

Lady Hardwick had already noticed her niece's tête-à-tête with Lord Courtney. In her preoccupation with her daughter's impending marriage, she had let the situation with her niece and Lord Courtney get out of hand, she feared. She must take action before it got further out of hand. She noticed Lord Satre standing at the far side of the ballroom, and a plan materialized in her mind. She walked purposefully over to him.

"Lord Satre, you are not dancing," she said. "Why do you not ask my niece?"

Lord Satre looked at Lady Hardwick in surprise. "I have already danced with her twice this evening, Lady Hardwick. If I were to dance with her again, the guests would assume there was an understanding between us."

"Yes," Lady Hardwick agreed, "but Letty is very ignorant of the rules of polite behavior. I doubt she realizes that."

Lord Satre smiled at Lady Hardwick with comprehension. The quality of that smile made Lady Hardwick feel momentarily uncomfortable, but she shrugged off the feeling. It was for her niece's own good that she was promoting a match with Lord Satre, whether the girl realized it or not.

Letty was reluctant to dance with Lord Satre a third time, but she feared that if she were to refuse him, her aunt would be angry. She allowed him to lead her onto the floor, thankful that the dance was one of the shorter ones. He said very little to her during the dance, but his smile made her uncomfortable. It seemed to indicate he was the possessor of some secret knowledge. She was relieved when he did not stay to talk after returning her to her aunt. Letty sat and began fanning herself vigorously, as though to blow away all memory of the distasteful dance.

"I am glad to see you took my advice about Lord Satre to heart," her aunt said sweetly, causing Letty to start and look at Lady Hardwick in surprise. "At least I assume you did so, for to dance three times in an evening with the same man implies the existence of an engagement, or the intent to become engaged."

Letty looked at her aunt in dismay. It could not be true! "At home I have danced many times in an evening with the same gentleman and no such assumption was made," she protested, although even as she spoke she realized that in London no man had ever sought her hand for a dance more than twice of an evening.

"In the country there is a lack of partners and no doubt it would be necessary. Unfortunately, as I have reminded you untold times, this is not Derbyshire. Your ignorance is no excuse. Unless you wish a great scandal to be brought upon us all, which I will not tolerate, you must accept Lord Satre as your intended."

Letty began to protest, but Lady Hardwick motioned her to silence as Sophie and Lord Lockwood joined them. A sense of panic came over Letty, and she scanned the room for Lord Courtney, wanting to appeal to him for help, but she did not see him anywhere. She would have gone to search for him, but Lady Hardwick, suspecting Letty's desire, claimed she was fatigued and insisted they leave early.

After a long and sleepless night, Letty determined to speak to Lady Hardwick about Lord Satre before callers started to arrive. Her aunt had refused to speak to her the night before, ordering her directly to bed. She found Lady Hardwick in the Grand Salon, and put forth an impassioned plea, but her aunt was deaf to her appeals.

"You cannot force me to become engaged to Lord Satre when Papa and Mama do not even know of it," Letty protested, using her last argument.

"They would expect me to do as I have done," Lady Hardwick said implacably. "They would wish me to do whatever is necessary to avert a scandal."

"Lord Satre," the footman announced, and the subject of their conversation entered the room. Letty looked at her unwelcome guest in despair and lapsed into silence, failing to answer his polite inquiries as to her health. He appeared not to notice her low spirits, however, and asked her to accompany him on a morning drive.

"That is kind of you, Lord Satre. I feel sure Laetitia should like to get out of the house into the fresh air," Lady Hardwick accepted for her niece. "Laetitia, get your hat and pelisse."

"Thank you, Lord Satre, but I am not feeling quite the thing," Letty said, hoping to escape the drive.

"Then the fresh air will do you good," Lady Hardwick insisted, looking at her niece meaningfully.

Letty reluctantly went to get her hat and pelisse. It occurred to her that perhaps she could use the occasion to tell Lord Satre she had been unaware of the implications of dancing three times of an evening with the same gentleman. Surely, if Lord Satre knew of her feelings, he would not press the issue. He could not wish to be engaged to someone who was unwilling.

Lord Satre was driving a small chaise that morning, and Letty was forced to sit very close to him. She moved as far over to the edge as she could, but was still uncomfortably near him. He drove to Hyde Park, and they joined the few morning visitors in the promenade about the ring. Letty felt her face turn crimson as she was forced to endure the knowing smiles of the people they met, who assumed the existence of an unannounced betrothal between her and Lord Satre. The discomfort she felt moved her to boldness.

"Lord Satre, might I speak with you?"

"Of course, but let us first go to a more private spot, where we shall not be overheard," he replied, directing the chaise to a side path. He drove a little distance down the path and stopped beneath the shade of a large tree.

"About what did you wish to speak with me?" he asked.

"Lord Satre," Letty began uncertainly, "I did not know, when I agreed to take the floor with you a third time last night, that it was not acceptable to do so in London. I have been told that here the acceptance of a third dance implies — that is, I would not like you to be under a misapprehension as to my feelings for you," she trailed off miserably.

"I am sorry to hear you say that," Lord Satre said slowly, "but at the time I took your action as a mark of favor and implied acceptance of my suit. Indeed, I had already spoken to your aunt and received her permission to pay my addresses to you. I thought by your acceptance of a third dance, you were indicating your intention to accept my suit," he lied plausibly.

"I am truly sorry if my behavior gave rise to false hopes," Letty said, "but I do not wish to be engaged to anyone at this time."

"That disappoints me, but I think you must allow that *I* did nothing wrong. Surely you do not wish me to look foolish in the eyes of Society because of your mistake. I am sure you know how uncomfortable that is," he added slyly. "To minimize any gossip, I ask simply that you do nothing. That is all. You need not confirm or deny the existence of an engagement between us.

You will continue to be seen in my company, but nothing will be announced officially. At the end of the Season, if nothing has been announced, Society will assume it died a natural death. That way both our reputations will be saved. I shall speak to your aunt and tell her of our decision when we return."

Letty did not like the idea, but felt it would be unreasonable of her to refuse. Much as she was repulsed by Lord Satre, she could not want to be the cause of his looking foolish in the eyes of Society. She knew only too well how that felt. It seemed odd that such a one as Lord Satre should be affected by anything Society might think or say, but then, what did she know of Society's power?

"Providing you understand my feelings."

"Thank you, my dear. Perhaps you might even change your mind." His gray eyes looked intently into her deep blue ones, and for some strange reason Letty felt unable to look away. His eyes seemed to glow and grow larger and larger, and suddenly she felt his lips clamp over hers. His action broke the spell, and Letty pulled away in revulsion.

"Lord Satre, I must ask you not to touch me again," she said indignantly, but not without a little fear as well.

"I am sorry, my dear, but your beauty overcame me," he said with a look that made Letty shiver. A gleam showed in his eyes, and Letty knew Lord Satre had seen her fear and relished it. She became aware of their isolation, and was contemplating jumping from the chaise and running, when she heard another vehicle coming down the road. Lord Satre picked up the reins and moved on with a smile at Letty that made her think he had known exactly what she had contemplated and found it amusing.

As soon as she arrived home, Letty ran directly to

her room. She went immediately to the washstand, and, taking the cloth, rubbed her lips vigorously, trying to remove the memory of Lord Satre's lips on hers. Then she flung herself on her bed and cried bitterly from disappointment that her first kiss should have been from the disgusting old Lord Satre.

That evening Letty pleaded a headache to avoid going out with her aunt and cousin. She wished to think over her predicament and decide what to do, but first she had to get rid of her maid. Daisy, believing that her mistress was ill, kept plying her with lavender water and tisanes. At last she was able to convince her that she needed only to rest alone awhile, and Daisy went to wait below until Letty should call.

Letty lay back in her pretty bed and pulled the pink coverlet up over her knees, resting her chin on her hands and trying to think her situation through. Although Lord Satre was not going to press for an official announcement, Letty feared that under pressure from her aunt she might somehow be forced into a betrothal. How alone she was, she thought, and then remembered Lady Wakeford. Of course! She could confide her problems to the older girl. Lady Wakeford, with her knowledge and experience of Society, could surely advise her.

Lady Hardwick did not object to Letty paying a call on Lady Wakeford the next morning, although she did instruct one of her footmen to accompany her niece. Letty supposed her aunt feared she might be planning to meet Lord Courtney.

Lady Wakeford was at home, and led Letty to a small salon when she asked if they might speak privately. Letty poured out her story to Lady Wakeford's sympathetic ears.

"Your aunt cannot *force* you to marry Lord Satre, Miss Biddle," she reassured her young friend at the end of her tale. "If the situation makes you uncomfortable, why do you not write to your mother and father and explain the whole to them?"

"At first I did not tell my parents of my problems here because I did not wish to worry them," Letty explained. "Then when I did attempt to tell them something of what was happening, they replied that I should obey my aunt. I fear my aunt's letters to them have given them the wrong idea of the situation, and I am afraid to tell them of Lord Satre lest they tell me to accept his suit," Letty finished unhappily.

"I cannot think, from what you have told me of your family, that your parents would do such a thing," Lady Wakeford replied, "but I do understand your concerns about Lord Satre. Let me think upon your problem, and I shall talk to you again. Meanwhile, try not to worry too much."

Lady Wakeford feared her words did not greatly ease her young friend's mind, but there was nothing else she could advise her to do. Letty thanked her for her counsel and left soon after. From the window of the salon, Lady Wakeford watched her leave, and mulled over the problem. She was still of the mind that Miss Biddle should confide the whole to her parents, but if she would not, no one could do it for her. That would constitute unwarranted interference in the Biddles' affairs. She decided to ask her brother's advice again. Perhaps this new development might inspire him to think of a way to assist Miss Biddle.

Jules returned home from his ride not long after, and was on his way upstairs when his sister called to him from the doorway of her dressing room.

"Jules, could I have a moment of your time?"

"Of course, Emily, what did you want?" Jules asked,

entering her room and taking a seat in a comfortable armchair. Emily seated herself nearby and repeated Miss Biddle's story.

"I tried to reassure her that her aunt cannot *force* her to marry Lord Satre," Lady Wakeford finished, "but I dislike seeing her so distressed. I should not be surprised if her aunt had a hand in the three dances with Lord Satre. It is not something that would occur unintentionally."

Jules frowned with distaste at the idea of an old lecher like Lord Satre possessing a beautiful young and innocent girl like Miss Biddle. "I suppose it is possible Lady Hardwick had something to do with it. From what I have seen of her behavior toward her niece, she does not appear to have any kind feelings toward Miss Biddle."

"I worry, too, that she may seek help from Lord Courtney," Lady Wakeford continued, "and that would not do."

"Because if Courtney knows of the pressure on her to accept Lord Satre, it may drive *him* to do something drastic so he does not lose Miss Biddle's fortune," Jules finished "Yes, I see it is quite a coil."

If only he had a legitimate reason to concern himself with Miss Biddle's affairs, Jules thought. Without one he was powerless to intercede, he realized, coming to the same conclusion his sister had earlier.

"I really fear there is little we can do," Jules said at length. "We have no right to meddle in her affairs or those of her family. I shall keep my eyes open and try to defuse any gossip I hear about Miss Biddle and Lord Satre, and you can do the same," he said, rising to leave.

With that, Lady Wakeford had to be satisfied.

Sophie had watched with mixed feelings the development of Lord Satre's interest in Letty. On one hand, it pleased her that her cousin was being pressured to accept the suit of someone she did not care for. On the other, Sophie did not actually want Letty to *marry* Lord Satre, for then Letty would outrank her since Lord Satre was a marquess. Lord Lockwood was only an earl. Sophie also sensed that there was the possibility of something developing between Lord Wakeford and her cousin. That would not do either, for Lord Wakeford was also a marquess.

Lord Courtney was another matter, however. Not only would Letty, as the wife of a viscount, be outranked by Sophie, as the wife of an earl, but Lord Courtney would quickly go through Letty's money and she would soon lose her fortune. Yes, of three possibilities, it would be best for Letty to marry Lord Courtney. How to promote that desirable outcome? Sophie decided to see if she could gain her cousin's confidence and perhaps a way would become clear.

Accordingly, she sought out her cousin in the library, where Letty spent much of her time. Letty reclined in the window seat, absorbed in a book. She looked up from her book in surprise at Sophie's step, for Sophie rarely sought out her company. Sophie seated herself next to Letty and spoke to her for a few minutes about books, even offering to lend Letty a new volume by Mrs. Radcliffe she had bought the previous week. These friendly overtures caused Letty to look at her cousin warily. She had not forgotten the incident of the red dress.

Sophie saw the wariness and instinctively knew how to overcome it. She slipped from her seat next to Letty and knelt at her cousin's feet, taking her cousin's hands in hers.

"Cousin Letty," she said, "I know that I have not always been kind to you since you arrived in London." She looked down as though in embarrassment. "I must confess to you that I was jealous. I know it was foolish, but I feared that your fortune might lure away some of my suitors. Now that I am engaged to Lord Lockwood, I know my fears were groundless, and I feel very bad about any unhappiness I may have caused you. Please forgive me and let us cry friends," she finished, looking up and willing a tear to trickle from her pale blue eyes.

Letty, although she was very surprised by her cousin's words, was more than willing to make a new start and be friends. It was what she had wished since she had first come to London.

"Of course I forgive you," she said, "although how someone as beautiful as you could have thought I would steal your suitors I cannot imagine." She pulled her cousin to her feet and embraced her.

As Sophie had hoped, her "confession" opened the way for them to share confidences, and before long Sophie had wheedled out the whole story of Letty's secret betrothal. She listened with a sympathetic expression on her face, trying to think how she might ensure Letty would marry Lord Courtney. A plea for advice opened the way.

"I think, Cousin Letty, that under the circumstances, the only possible recourse open to you is an elopement."

"Elopement?" Letty echoed in a shocked voice. "I could not do that. Lady Wakeford urged me to write my parents and tell them the whole, and I have been thinking perhaps I should do that. I feel when my mother and father know all, they will not press me to accept Lord Satre."

"But will your parents allow you to marry Lord Courtney? My mother will tell them he is a gazetted fortune hunter and to forbid it," Sophie said shrewdly. "Who will your mother and father listen to, you or Mama?"

Letty was silent. She had not thought of that. It was true her parents were more likely to give credence to her aunt's words. Still, she could not like the idea of an elopement. It was so ramshackle. She wished to have a proper betrothal—the banns read at church, a special gown made, her trousseau purchased, vows taken before her family and friends.

Sophie saw Letty's hesitation and offered to have a note carried to Lord Courtney to arrange a meeting that Letty might discuss the problem with him. Sophie was shrewd enough to know that Lord Courtney would be likely to endorse her plan of an elopement. Were Letty's parents to have time to investigate Lord Courtney's background, they would refuse to consider his suit.

Letty agreed, brightening at the thought of seeing Lord Courtney. Surely he would take her position and explain to Sophie why they could not elope. Letty might even be able to persuade him to go to Derbyshire and speak to her father, before the end of the Season.

Chapter Nine

It was a simple matter for Sophie to arrange a meeting with Lord Courtney. Sophie's maid, Polly, was of a romantic disposition, and more than willing to secretly deliver notes to a handsome gentleman. The meeting was set for the library, since Lady Hardwick had no taste for reading and never accompanied her daughter there.

When they arrived at the library at the appointed time, they found Lord Courtney was already there. Sophie borrowed one book, and the three left the library together. They walked slowly around Berkeley Square, Polly following at a distance. Letty explained to Lord Courtney that she had confided their betrothal to Sophie, but she was reluctant to broach Sophie's idea of an elopement. Sophie was not so reticent.

"I told Cousin Letty that an elopement is the only answer to your predicament," she said, turning to face Lord Courtney and observe his reaction to her suggestion. Lord Courtney caught her gaze, and a look of understanding and complicity passed between them. Lord Courtney realized that Sophie, for whatever her reasons, had decided to promote the attachment between himself and Miss Biddle. He recognized that an elopement was the best plan, considering his reputation. If Miss Biddle's father were to look into his circumstances before a wedding took place, he would be likely to forbid the match. If he were presented with a marriage that had already taken place, he would put his daughter's happiness first and accept it. Lord Courtney counted on that same love for his daughter to open the purse strings before his daughter came of age. Squire Biddle would not wish his daughter to live in poverty.

"I told Cousin Sophie that I felt an elopement was too drastic a measure, and that I should confide the whole to my mother and father," Letty interposed, hoping that Lord Courtney would agree with her.

Lord Courtney frowned and appeared to be thinking the situation over. "I cannot like the necessity of such a course, but I fear your cousin is correct," he said at last. "Your parents no doubt still consider you a child and will tell you to do as your aunt advises. We must present them with a *fait accompli*."

Letty still did not like the idea, but coming from Lord Courtney, it did not seem quite so reprehensible. "Think of the scandal when people find out," she protested weakly.

"The scandal will not last," Lord Courtney reassured her. "What do we care for Society's opinion? We shall purchase an estate in the country and settle there. Is that not what you would prefer, Letty?"

Letty blushed at his use of her diminutive. The idea of living in the country with Lord Courtney was very appealing. She looked at him, so splendid in his form-fitting buckskins and morning coat, and felt her heart begin to race.

They were nearing Upper St. James's Park, and being quite aware how his presence affected Letty, Lord Courtney decided to take the matter into his own hands.

"Would you allow me to speak with your cousin privately one moment?" he asked Sophie.

Sophie agreed, and dropped back with Polly. Lord Courtney led Letty into the park to a secluded spot by some bushes. There he stopped and took her hands in his.

"I know you cannot like the necessity of an elopement," he said, "but I feel it is the only way if you do indeed wish to become my wife. You *do* wish that, Letty?" He looked intently into her eyes, and saw by the color mounting in her face that she was not immune to his appeal.

Letty felt herself weakening. Lord Courtney pressed her hands in his and drew her forward, placing his lips over hers. Letty melted. This was more what she had thought a kiss would be. His lips were warm and firm, and their touch made her feel light-headed. She responded tentatively to his kiss, and then, remembering where they were, pulled away.

"We are betrothed," Lord Courtney reminded her, looking at her tenderly and lightly caressing her face.

"If you think an elopement is the only way," Letty capitulated.

"I do," Lord Courtney replied firmly. He placed one more light kiss upon her lips and led her back to find Sophie, who was waiting impatiently for their return.

"We haven't too much time," Sophie cautioned. "We still need to work out the details. I think it would be best to make your departure from Vauxhall. I shall get up a party. Mama does not like Vauxhall, and if I choose the guests carefully, she will not find it necessary to accompany us. I shall arrange to have a note delivered to Letty, asking her to join some other friends, and you can have a carriage waiting at the entrance."

Lord Courtney looked at Sophie with admiration. It was obvious she had worked it all out earlier. "An excellent idea, Miss Hardwick. When you have decided upon the date, let me know, and I shall make my arrangements. Until then," he said to Letty, and with a bow and last tender look, he left.

As the night of the planned Vauxhall elopement approached, Letty felt sure her increasing agitation would make her aunt suspicious. Although Sophie and Lord Courtney had convinced her the elopement was the only way she would be able to marry, Letty still could not feel it was right. She knew her parents would disapprove, as would her only friend, Lady Wakeford. Thoughts of Lady Wakeford brought thoughts of Lord Wakeford to mind, and Letty felt that if he knew of her plans, he would not have that familiar smile of amusement on his face, but a frown of severe disapprobation.

All too soon the night arrived. Sophie had engineered the Vauxhall excursion well. Lady Hardwick, who did not like the Gardens, thinking too many commoners were to be seen there, was easily persuaded by her daughter that her chaperonage would not be necessary in a party to consist of Lord Lockwood, Miss Alcock and her brother, and Lord Rutherford.

Letty was very quiet during the ride to the Gardens, but no one paid any heed. She wondered what Daisy would think when she did not return. Would she be blamed? Sophie had insisted that the maid not be let into their plans. Letty was taking nothing with her but the clothes on her back.

Letty was so nervous over the impending elopement that she did not appreciate the beauty of the Gardens in the least, although it was the first time she had seen them. She walked unseeingly along the neat graveled walks lined by trees and high hedges, past enticing grottoes, shining white statues, and tinkling cascades.

They hired a supper box with a gilded front looking directly onto the Promenade, and ordered the powdered beef and wine-laced custards for which the Gardens were famous. The rest of the party ate with relish and watched the people parading by, but Letty could barely swallow a thing, so tight had her throat become with nervousness.

Sophie, who was familiar with Vauxhall, had planned the details of the elopement carefully in order that no one's suspicions should be raised. When the Master of the Box came to inform their party that the waterworks were about to begin, a servant came up with a message purportedly from Lady Wakeford, requesting that Letty join her party for the waterworks.

Sophie encouraged Letty to accept the bogus invitation, and Letty agreed, excusing herself from the others and following the man away. The remainder of the party thought nothing of the incident, knowing that Lady Wakeford was indeed a friend of Miss Biddle's. If Lady Wakeford had caught sight of her in the Gardens, it was natural she would wish to speak with her friend.

As Letty followed the servant toward the entrance of the Gardens, her reluctance to go through with the elopement increased. The step was so *final*. Now that the moment was upon her, she felt she could not do such a thing to her family. She would explain her change of heart to Lord Courtney and beg him to come up with a less drastic plan. They had reached the entrance, and Letty saw a waiting carriage with pulled blinds. The servant opened the carriage door for Letty, and then jumped up with the driver.

Letty put her foot on the bottom step, planning to get in and talk with Lord Courtney, when she was overcome by a premonition and pulled back. Her action caused Lord Courtney to emerge from the carriage.

"What is the problem, Letty?" he asked. "Everything is set. We must go immediately so we shall have enough of a head start that no one will be able to overtake us."

Letty wavered at the coaxing voice, but some inner strength kept her firm.

"No, Lord Courtney, I cannot go through with it. It simply is not right."

"Nonsense, you are only nervous. That is understandable," Lord Courtney reassured her. He took her by the arm and attempted to draw her toward the carriage.

Letty, however, continued to refuse. "No, Lord Courtney. I have thought it over. Such an extreme solution to our circumstances is not necessary. My aunt cannot *force* me to marry Lord Satre, and I feel sure my parents will allow us to marry once they meet you."

Lord Courtney did not take so sanguine a view.

"We cannot be sure of that," he said a little impatiently. "What we *can* be sure of is that your aunt will distort the truth because she wishes you to accept Lord Satre's suit." Again he took her arm and tried to pull her toward the carriage.

"No!" Letty cried, beginning to feel alarmed at his insistence, and attempting to pull out of his grasp. This was not the gentle and charming Lord Courtney she had known, but a frightening stranger.

"Enough nonsense. We have no time to waste," Lord Courtney said, a menacing tone to his voice, and he signaled the servant who had led Letty to the carriage to come to his assistance. He jumped down from the carriage and took Letty's other arm, and together they forced her toward the carriage.

Jules looked around the ballroom with boredom, finding that even the wit of the Beau was palling. He began to wish he had gone with some other friends who had asked him to join a party to Vauxhall. He had refused the invitation and accompanied his sister to the ball, hoping to see Miss Biddle there, but she was nowhere in sight.

"Wakeford, have you gone deaf?" the Beau inquired languidly. "You have become quite dull of late. If it were not for your impeccable taste in attire, I should refuse to be seen in your company."

"My thoughts were elsewhere," Jules acknowledged.

"In the country?" the Beau asked shrewdly. "It occurs to me that your abstraction dates from a certain evening that Miss *L.L.* danced three times with Lord *S.* However, I must agree with you that the evening is quite dull. I think I shall repair to White's. Care to join me, Wakeford?"

"No, I think I shall join some friends at Vauxhall," Jules replied, and, taking his leave of the Beau, went to find his host and make his excuses.

Knowing that he would be able to get a ride home with his friends, he left his carriage for his sister and mother and took a hackney. He got out at the entrance on the Vauxhall road, and was walking toward the doors when he heard raised voices, one of them a woman's. Looking in the direction the voices were coming from, he saw what appeared to be an altercation in progress. Thinking that the woman might be in need of assistance but wishing to be sure it was not just an argument between a gentleman and his light-o'-love, Jules approached them quietly, staying in the shadows. As he got closer, he realized with shock that the woman was Miss Biddle. He saw two men attempt to force her toward a carriage with pulled blinds, and decided he must intervene.

"I believe Miss Biddle does not desire to accompany you," he said, stepping out of the shadows.

"This is none of your affair, Wakeford," snarled Lord Courtney, turning at the sound of Lord Wakeford's voice but not releasing his hold on Letty.

"I am making it my affair. It is always a gentleman's affair when a lady is being forced to do something against her will," Jules replied calmly, casually pulling his swordstick partway out.

The servant had let go of Letty's arm, but Lord Courtney did not, although he saw he was defeated. He cursed himself inwardly for his failure to bring his pistol with him when he left the carriage. His fury at having his plans thwarted at the last minute moved him to speak unguardedly.

"Lady," he sneered. "She is no more than a simple squire's daughter made acceptable by the amount of

152

her fortune, despite its being tainted by trade."

Even in the dim light of the lamps Jules could see Miss Biddle shrink at the heartless words, and it infuriated him.

"Release her at once," he said, threat implicit in his voice. Lord Courtney released Letty's arm, and she ran to Lord Wakeford.

"My seconds will call upon you this evening, Courtney," Lord Wakeford said as Lord Courtney went back to his carriage.

"My pleasure," Lord Courtney replied, giving a mock bow and leaping into the carriage. He thought briefly of retrieving the pistol and trying to take Letty by force, but realized he was likely to be interrupted by other pleasurers in the attempt. He shouted an order to the driver, and the carriage raced away.

Letty stood wordlessly, watching the carriage and Lord Courtney disappear into the night. She was stunned by the happenings of the past few minutes. The import of Lord Wakeford's last words to Lord Courtney did not penetrate her consciousness. She was aware only that she had been a great fool, and that the others who had warned her that Lord Courtney wanted her for her money only had been correct. Worse, Lord Wakeford had been there to witness her shame, although if he had not, she thought, shuddering, she would have been forced to go with Lord Courtney against her will. She turned with outward calm to Lord Wakeford.

"Thank you for your assistance, Lord Wakeford. I am greatly indebted to you."

Lord Wakeford ignored her thanks. "Do you feel

153

composed enough to rejoin your friends? I presume you did come to Vauxhall with a party?"

"Yes," Letty replied, "I came with my cousin Sophie, Lord Lockwood, and Mr. and Miss Alcock. They hired a box on the Promenade."

"I shall escort you back to them," he said, taking her hand and leading her gently back into the Gardens.

The waterworks were over, and her party back in their box. Sophie looked at Letty questioningly when she returned in the company of Lord Wakeford, but the others saw nothing strange in her return. They assumed she had been with Lady Wakeford, and it was natural that Lord Wakeford would escort her back to the box.

Lord Lockwood invited Jules to join the party for a glass of punch, which he accepted. He entertained the party with amusing anecdotes, and Letty saw that he was exerting himself to be entertaining to draw attention from her until she had time to completely compose herself. After a half hour, Lord Wakeford excused himself to rejoin his own party, and Sophie and her party left the Gardens to return home.

When they reached the town house, Sophie followed Letty to her bedchamber instead of going upstairs. She peremptorily ordered Daisy from the room and closed the door behind her.

"What went wrong?" she demanded. "Why did you return with Lord Wakeford? Wasn't Lord Courtney there?"

"Yes, he was there," Letty replied, and in a flat, unemotional voice she recounted the events of the evening. "So you see, he was interested in me only because of my money after all," she finished.

Sophie went through rapid changes of emotion as Letty told her tale. At first she was unhappy that her plan to bring disgrace upon Letty by an elopement had failed, but by the end of Letty's story she realized that this presented an even better opportunity to disgrace her cousin. No one could survive the shame and disgrace of having a duel fought over them.

"Do you understand that Lord Wakeford and Lord Courtney are to fight a duel over you? If it gets out, there will be a great scandal," she said with relish.

"A duel?" Letty repeated, looking at her cousin blankly.

"What did you think having his seconds call upon Lord Courtney meant?"

A cold fear came over Letty as the import of Sophie's words finally penetrated. A duel! One of them might be killed! Although she had been deeply hurt by Lord Courtney's unkind words, she did not wish him dead, and as for the thought of Lord Wakeford being killed, it was not to be borne.

"We must stop them," she said in great agitation. "What can we do, Sophie?"

"It is not possible to stop them," Sophie informed her gleefully. "It is a matter of honor now."

"I must go to the Wakeford's and try," Letty insisted, putting on her cloak again, and pulling the hood over her head.

"It is too late at night for you to make a call on the Wakefords," Sophie objected.

"I must go anyway," Letty insisted. "Lady Wakeford will speak to me."

Sophie shrugged. "If you insist. I shall wait here until your return," she said, settling into a chair.

The footman who answered the Wakefords' door hesitated at first to let Letty in, but then recognized her from her previous calls. He had her wait a moment in the entrance hall while he informed Lady Wakeford of her unusual late-night caller, and returned shortly to show Letty into a small salon off the hall. Lady Wakeford joined her almost immediately.

"What is amiss?" she asked, seeing her friend's distressed face.

"Lady Wakeford, you must stop your brother. He plans to fight a duel," Letty cried, and poured out the whole story of the elopement. "Sophie says you cannot stop them, but you *must!*" she finished in a despairing tone.

Lady Wakeford did not make an immediate answer as she pondered what to do. She felt partly responsible herself since she was the one who had urged her brother to protect Miss Biddle from Lord Courtney. Although she recognized that her brother would have intervened to save any young woman from such a predicament, he would not necessarily have challenged the man to a duel. She also knew that her brother could not be dissuaded from any course he felt touched his honor.

"I fear your cousin is correct," she said at last. "There is no way to prevent the duel from taking place."

"But he might be killed. Could your mother stop it, or the authorities?"

"You do not understand about gentleman and dueling," Lady Wakeford explained. "It would do no good to try to stop the duel. If he were to know his family was aware of the duel, it might only prey on his mind and rob him of his concentration. No, I shall not tell my mother or try to stop the duel, and you must not either. Do not worry," she said as Letty looked ready to cry, "Jules is an accomplished marksman."

"The authorities," Letty repeated.

"We cannot inform the authorities," Lady Wakeford said with finality. "It would not be the thing."

Lady Wakeford's words did little to reassure Letty. Lady Wakeford, thinking that perhaps Letty's distress was partly for fear Lord Courtney might be killed, or fear for her reputation should the story get about, tried again to reassure her young friend.

"My brother will not kill Lord Courtney, I feel certain, and the fact of the duel will be kept quiet. Dueling is against the law, and those involved will not broadcast their involvement."

"I am not worried about my reputation," Letty said impatiently. "Lord Courtney has shown in his usage of me that he is an unscrupulous person. It is for Lord Wakeford that I fear."

Lady Wakeford looked at Letty sharply, wondering if Miss Biddle's concern sprang from gratitude, guilt, or perhaps a deeper feeling for her brother than she had hitherto suspected. She went to Letty and placed her arm around her, speaking to her seriously.

"If you are concerned about my brother, you must do as I ask. Return home and say nothing to anyone. I shall send a note as soon as Jules returns from the duel. I would suspect it will be held early in the morning. I cannot find out for certain, for I doubt he will return home until the duel is over. I promise that as soon as I hear the result, I shall send you word."

Letty saw the good sense of Lady Wakeford's advice, and returned home, accompanied by one of the Wakefords' footmen. She found Sophie waiting to be told the result of her call, and told her of Lady Wakeford's insistence that she do nothing to try to stop the duel. This news satisfied Sophie, and she went up to her bedchamber to lie awake and figure out how best to spread the tale of the duel. Letty also lay awake, unable to sleep from fear for the safety of the combatants.

Chapter Ten

After leaving Letty's party at Vauxhall, Jules went to search for his friends. He found them enjoying supper in a Chinese-style kiosk. He was glad to see that Lord Palmer was of the party, for the rules of dueling required that one's seconds be one's equal in rank, and Lord Jeffrey Palmer qualified. He managed to get Lord Palmer aside and put his request to him. Lord Palmer was surprised to find his friend involved in a duel, but readily agreed to act as his second. They made their excuses to the rest of the party and repaired to Lord Palmer's town house. There was a great deal to be done before the duel could take place, and Jules did not wish to return home, where his mother or sister might become suspicious of the activity.

It was the responsibility of the seconds to attempt a reconciliation between Lord Courtney and Lord Wakeford, but as Lord Palmer expected, their attempts were futile. Lord Courtney was too angry, knowing that his outburst had lost him any hope of persuading Letty to marry him, and he was determined Wakeford would pay dearly for his loss. Jules would not forgive Lord Courtney's remarks about

159

Miss Biddle unless he would apologize, which Lord Courtney refused to do. It only remained, then, for the seconds to work out the details of the duel. Lord Courtney, as the challenged, had the right to choose the meeting place and weapons, Jules the distance.

As he waited at Lord Palmer's residence for his friend to return, Jules wondered what weapon Courtney would choose—swords or pistols. He thought of the mahogany box of dueling pistols, their butts beautifully inlaid with silver wire, reposing in his study desk at his town house. He had never used them. Although dueling was illegal, the law was generally ignored, and every gentleman had to be proficient in the art of defending himself in case he was called out. Jules thought Courtney would choose pistols, although he himself would prefer swords. More luck was involved with pistols—the best did not shoot straight. However, he was proficient in the use of both, and decided not to worry.

Lord Palmer returned in a half hour with the information that Courtney had chosen pistols at Hyde Park. Jules considered a moment, and then chose ten yards as the distance. Lord Palmer left once again, to meet with Courtney's second and set the times and terms of firing now that the weapon, place, and distance had been determined. Lord Palmer also contacted a surgeon he knew he could trust not to inform the authorities of the proposed duel. He returned some two hours later to tell Jules all was arranged, and that the time had been set for four in the morning.

All the things that needed to be done were done,

and Palmer sent for a bottle of Madeira. Jules accepted one glass, but drank of it sparingly, for the duel was scarcely five hours hence, and he wished to have a clear head. The friends settled into chairs at opposite sides of the fire and stared into the flames, each with their own thoughts.

"Do you think Courtney can be trusted?" Lord Palmer said suddenly, voicing a concern he had had since he first learned of the duel. Lord Courtney did not have a good reputation, and Palmer feared he might not play by the rules.

"I doubt he will dare cheat with the seconds, surgeons, and servants all there to witness his actions," Jules replied.

The two friends lapsed into silence again, and after a while Lord Palmer excused himself to get some sleep. Jules refused a bed, saying he would catch what sleep he needed in the chair. Lord Palmer did not argue, knowing that each man must prepare for a duel as he thought best.

After his friend left the room, Jules relaxed more deeply into the comfortably upholstered armchair. It was somehow fitting that the first duel he would fight was to defend the honor of the girl he had given an uncharitable nickname. He wondered briefly if Miss Biddle would try to stop the duel or inform his mother or sister of it, and then decided it was unlikely. He was not even positive she had understood a duel was to take place.

He picked up his glass of Madeira again and held it before him, watching the reflections of the firelight in the faceted glass. It crossed his mind that this might be his last glass, that he might die shortly, but he did not allow himself to dwell upon the possibility. What would happen would happen, he thought fatalistically.

When Jules and Lord Palmer arrived at the meeting place in Hyde Park in the early morning, Lord Courtney, his second, and the surgeons were already there. As Jules got out of the carriage, he noted the park was unusually still. There was no wind at all, and at the early morning hour it was eerily silent. Everything was gray—the sky, grass, trees, and people all melded into a uniform leaden tint.

The pistols were Lord Courtney's, and the seconds checked them carefully to be sure the flints were adjusted and all was in working order. They then loaded them in each other's presence and gave them to the principals. Jules noted briefly the pistol was a Parker. The silver inlaid butt felt smooth and heavy in his hand. He looked at Courtney, who was talking to his second. He appeared to be rather nervous.

All was ready. The ground was marked out, and the seconds retired eight yards from the line of fire. The two surgeons stood waiting two yards behind the seconds, and the drivers and other servants in a line farther back.

Jules and Lord Courtney stood with their sides toward each other in order to provide the smallest target and so their arms would help shield their bodies in case they were hit. There was absolute silence from all the spectators as they waited for the signal to fire. To his surprise, now that the moment had actually arrived, Jules found he felt no fear whatsoever, only a cold, calm resolve and a sense of inevitability.

The signal was given, and to the shock of the spectators, who took a moment to realize what had happened, Lord Courtney anticipated the signal by a fraction of a second and fired early. His bullet whizzed unnoticed by Lord Wakeford's head. Jules, who had intended to fire above Courtney's head, instead responded instinctively to the premature shot and fired. Lord Courtney's pistol dropped to the ground as Jules's bullet hit its mark. He staggered and clasped his right shoulder with his left hand.

Jules stood a moment after his bullet struck Courtney, his arm falling to his side, the pistol dangling from his hand. The surgeons ran to attend Lord Courtney, and Lord Palmer went over to Jules, taking the pistol and telling his friend that Lord Courtney was not badly injured. The participants began to hasten to their vehicles, and within minutes all had vanished from the park. Duels had to be conducted swiftly lest the authorities got wind of them and showed up, taking all into custody.

As Jules and Lord Palmer rode home, they did not speak of the duel, but of trivialities, as though they were returning together from a late ball. Lord Palmer delivered Jules to his town house, and Jules clasped his friend's hand briefly but warmly to show his thanks before getting down from the carriage.

He let himself into the house and went slowly upstairs to his bedchamber. Now that it was over, reaction was setting in, and he felt the need for a glass of spirits. To his surprise, he found his sister asleep in a chair by his fire.

"I could not dissuade her from waiting for you," his valet informed him in a whisper, and Jules knew

Emily must have heard of the duel. He dismissed his valet and went to awaken his sister, gently shaking her by her shoulder. Her eyes flew open and she stood up, tearfully embracing him.

"Where did you hear of the duel?"

"Miss Biddle came last night to tell me of it and try to get me to stop it," Emily explained, gaining control over her emotions.

"You did not try to stop it?" Jules questioned, loosening his cravat and taking off his coat. He went to a table where a decanter of port stood, and poured himself a generous glass.

"I had every confidence in your skill," she said, sitting back down in her chair. "I also knew I would be unable to talk you out of it and feared that were I to worry you about it, it might disturb your concentration and do more harm than good."

Jules smiled and relaxed into a chair near Emily's, marveling at the wisdom his younger sister had exhibited.

"I see you are uninjured," Emily continued matter-of-factly. "How is Lord Courtney?"

"I struck him in the arm. I do not think you need worry about his troubling Miss Biddle again. I make no doubt he will soon head for the Continent," he predicted, raising his glass to his lips again as he thought of Courtney's inevitable disgrace when the story of his premature firing spread.

"By the way," he added, "I hope you impressed upon Miss Biddle the necessity of keeping quiet about the duel. Should the circumstances of the duel get about, it would do her credit no good."

"Yes, I did instruct her not to tell anyone of it, although she had already told her cousin." A thought occurred to her. "It is strange that Miss Hardwick is suddenly friendly with Miss Biddle. Miss Biddle told me that her cousin had helped plan the elopement with Lord Courtney."

Jules looked at her thoughtfully. "I had wondered about that. It was not like Miss Biddle to agree to anything as ramshackle as an elopement. Her mistakes have stemmed from ignorance, not a lack of propriety. I suppose Lord Courtney and Miss Hardwick persuaded her of its necessity. Although why Miss Hardwick should wish her cousin to do so, I cannot imagine."

"Jealousy," Emily stated perceptively. "Although I shall miss her, I shall be glad to see Miss Biddle return to Derbyshire when the Season is at an end," his sister confessed. "She is not happy in London."

Jules had not thought of Miss Biddle's leaving before, and the idea was oddly unwelcome. Surely he could not be coming to have an attachment to the chit? No, that was not possible. He was an intimate of the Beau, a leader of fashion. He could not possibly care for a simple squire's daughter of no polish or wit. Could he?

Letty lay awake the whole night, wondering when the duel would be, or if it was already over. What if Lord Wakeford were lying on the ground wounded that very minute? Or worse. It would be her fault.

It occurred to her that she was more worried about Lord Wakeford than about Lord Courtney, although she could not wish either of them to be hurt despite Lord Courtney's last cruel words. Lord Wakeford, though, was acting in her defense. Defense of her foolishness, she realized miserably. Why hadn't she listened to her aunt, or to her friend, Lady Wakeford, when they had tried to warn her that he was a fortune hunter? But no, she had allowed her resentment toward her aunt for her criticisms of her behavior to cloud her sense of duty toward her sponsor. She had been so desperate for a gentleman of Society to show her approval that she had been unwilling to listen to her older and wiser friend. What a headstrong, ignorant child she had been! She wished she had never come to London. She should have stayed in Derbyshire, where she belonged.

Letty alternately lay in bed staring at the ceiling and paced the room, checking the clock incessantly. How slowly the time passed! When the sky began to gray with the dawn, her agitation increased. Why had she not heard from Lady Wakeford?

Finally, at eight o'clock a servant tapped on the door. Letty answered it herself and snatched the note from the girl, causing the maid to look at her strangely before she left, but Letty paid her no heed. She tore the note open and hastily scanned the contents. It gave no details, but stated simply that the duel was over and both principals well. Letty sighed with relief and fell into her bed with exhaustion, sleeping until long past midday.

If it had not been for Sophie, the story of the duel would not have gotten out. Lord Courtney did not wish the story of his premature firing to get about; Lord Wakeford and the seconds were too honorable to speak of the duel, since it involved a young woman of good family; the servants who had witnessed it valued their places too much to bruit it about.

But Sophie thought the opportunity to ruin her cousin was too good to let pass. With Lord Courtney now out of the picture, Letty would be likely to marry Lord Satre or even Lord Wakeford, and that would not do. She would *not* have her cousin outrank her, and the only way she could see to prevent it was to disgrace Letty so thoroughly in the eyes of Society that none but a cit would look at her, even with her fortune.

She would have to be careful, however, how she spread the news about. If she told her mother, Lady Hardwick would undoubtedly forbid her to spread the story. Her mother would worry that some of the disgrace might attach to her. Sophie, secure in her betrothal to Lord Lockwood, did not fear Letty's behavior would affect her standing in Society.

Sophie decided she would tell a few select friends, in strictest confidence, of course, about the circumstances of the duel, leaving her involvement out. There was no one to gainsay her, and no better way to ensure that a story spread quickly through Society than to tell it to someone in strictest confidence. She would begin with a morning call on Miss Alcock.

Sophie's plan worked well. In less than one day the story was known throughout Society. The tale caused Lord Wakeford's credit to go up, but Letty's plummeted. Invitations to Letty to attend functions still came to the house on Adam Street, but Society no longer attempted to hide its scorn of the provincial with the fortune from trade. The consensus was that Miss Biddle should be grateful for the chance to associate with the *ton,* no matter how impolitely she was treated.

In the week that followed the duel, Letty noticed that the better quality of her suitors had vanished. Even young Lord Arlington, who had been one of her most faithful admirers, now did not ask her for even a single dance. The only ones who still pursued her were those with less than noble connections, or those desperate for money. The latter seemed to think they were doing her a favor by paying her attention, even if they did it only because of her money. One even told her so when he made her an offer of marriage, not bothering to go through her aunt. The only exception was Lord Satre, and Letty *wished* he would follow the example of the others.

Lady Hardwick was extremely upset over the affair, and did not allow Letty to go anywhere without her chaperonage. After a musical evening during which Lady Hardwick had overheard some women saying that she would *never* be able to marry her niece to a gentleman of quality now, Lady Hardwick summoned Letty to her dressing room.

"I have decided that after the disgraceful affair of the duel, it is time an official announcement were made of your betrothal to Lord Satre."

"I do not wish to marry Lord Satre," Letty insisted. "The duel is no reason to change my mind." Letty had hoped Lady Hardwick had forgotten about her intention to marry her off to Lord Satre, and was distressed to find she had been mistaken.

"Do you not understand that the duel has

changed everything?" Lady Hardwick said sternly. "No one else will even consider marrying you now." Perhaps, she thought privately, *one* good thing might come from the whole disgraceful affair if she could use it to force her niece to accept Lord Satre.

"That is not true," Letty said bitterly. "I am sure my money will attract some gentleman. In fact, Lord Shackleton offered for me yesterday."

"Lord Shackleton is a gazetted fortune hunter," Lady Hardwick said. "I promised your mother I would not allow you to marry a fortune hunter. That leaves only Lord Satre."

"I will not marry Lord Satre," Letty said quietly but firmly.

Her aunt looked at her angrily. "I have had enough of your defiance. Did you not learn anything from your experience with Lord Courtney? If you cannot obey me, I think it time you return home to Derbyshire."

"If you wish, Aunt," Letty replied quietly, inwardly delighted. There was nothing for her in London now. Lord Courtney had been exposed, and Lord Wakeford would never care to see her again after witnessing her disgrace, she was sure.

Lady Hardwick had not planned to really send Letty home, but now that she had said it, it seemed to be the best idea. Sophie was engaged, and no one could say she had not done the best she could for her niece. All in all, it had come out well, except for the slight disgrace attached to them by their connection to Letty. Even there, Lady Hardwick felt, Society must excuse her, as it was obvious no one could have controlled such a wayward provincial as her niece. The only thing that still upset her was the loss of the money promised to her by Lord Satre if she had persuaded her niece to accept his suit.

Still, perhaps it was true that money was not everything. She disliked being under the scrutiny of Society, and would be glad to have her niece gone from her house. The sooner she was gone, the sooner Society would find another *on-dit* to replace the one about her niece. Letty's presence had already gained her the entree to the homes of some of the better *ton,* and now her daughter's engagement to Lord Lockwood would ensure they remained open. No, she had no further use for her niece. It was better she leave.

Chapter Eleven

Letty looked out the carriage window at the familiar soft hills and gentle rises of the Derbyshire countryside with an anticipation surpassing even that with which she had viewed the unfamiliar streets of London two months before. Home! She could hardly wait to arrive. Oh, to see her father and mother again and be among people who accepted her as she was!

Once the decision had been made for Letty to return home, her aunt had lost no time in arranging it. Since her father's carriage and coachman had returned to Derbyshire after bringing her to London, and her aunt did not wish to wait for it to return, Lady Hardwick had arranged to hire one to carry Letty home. She had no intention of sending the carriage she had purchased with the squire's money back with her niece. The squire might keep it. She felt it was little enough compensation for the grief her niece had caused her during her stay.

Letty had helped Daisy pack the trunks, taking all her new clothes, both the ones her aunt had selected and the ones she had ordered herself. The former she planned to give to Daisy; the neutral colors would look attractive on the maid with her bright red hair.

Letty's departure from London had been arranged so swiftly that she had had time to pay only a short call on the dowager countess and Lady Wakeford to bid them good-bye and thank them for their kindness. Her friend had seemed genuinely sorry to see her go, and it was the only moment when Letty herself felt a pang at leaving London.

"Please come and visit me in Derbyshire, Lady Wakeford," she had begged, and given Lady Wakeford her address so they could correspond.

"I shall try. And I promise to write often," Lady Wakeford had said, embracing her friend. Lord Wakeford had not been at home, and Letty asked his sister to make her farewells for her.

Her parting from her aunt and cousin had been far less affecting. Sophie had not even bothered to get up early to bid her good-bye, and her aunt's farewell had been markedly cool. Letty forced herself to thank her aunt for the Season and had gotten into the carriage feeling only relief at the thought of never again entering the town house on Adam Street.

A familiar turning of the road brought Letty's thoughts back to the present, and she watched eagerly, waiting for the first sight of her Derbyshire home. When the low-pitched roof of gray slate came into view, her heart began to beat fast with anticipation and she felt tears of happiness fill her eyes.

"We are almost home, Daisy," she told her maid excitedly.

Daisy's eyes, which had been closing with sleep, opened wide, and she joined Letty in looking out the window. "I'm that glad to be back, miss," she confided to her mistress.

"I am, too," Letty agreed. When the carriage halted before the house, Letty did not even wait for the carriage door to be opened, but pulled it open herself, jumped down to the ground, and ran eagerly to the front door and into the stone-paved entrance hall. At the sound of the door her parents came into the hall. Letty threw herself into her father's arms, where she unaccountably burst into tears.

Squire Biddle patted his daughter's glossy curls awkwardly, saying, "There, there, it's all right, puss, you are safe at home now." He met his wife's eyes above Letty's head, and Mrs. Biddle shook her head slightly, indicating that now was not the time.

The squire and his wife had been awaiting their daughter's arrival with trepidation. The news in the letters from Lady Hardwick had caused them great uneasiness, and their daughter's letters had not relieved it. Letty's correspondence had seemed restrained and very unlike her since she had been in London. The last letter from Lady Hardwick, informing them of the duel and Letty's impending return home, had greatly distressed them both.

Letty went from her father's arms to her mother's. After she embraced her daughter warmly, Mrs. Biddle led her upstairs to her bedchamber above the hall and urged her to rest from her journey. She and her husband would have to have a serious talk with Letty, but it could wait until later.

* * *

The next morning Letty awoke to the sun pouring unfettered through the bedchamber windows, and a warm sense of peace filled her. She rang for Daisy, who came in carrying a tray with a thick dark wheaten loaf and milk.

"Mrs. Biddle bade me to bring your breakfast to you, and I thought you would like this," she said shyly.

Letty bit into the coarse bread with relish. "It's delicious, Daisy. It will be good to eat Mrs. Perry's cooking again."

Daisy agreed with her mistress wholeheartedly. When Letty finished her breakfast, Daisy helped her dress in one of her new gowns from London, and Letty gave her young maid the ones Lady Hardwick had chosen for her. As Daisy exclaimed over her mistress's generous gift, Letty thought she may as well go down and face her parents. They would be waiting for explanations, she felt sure.

She found them together in the same parlor where she had pleaded so ardently for a London Season four months earlier.

"That is a becoming gown," her mother said after they bade each other good morning. "I shall be interested to see your other gowns and hear of the latest London fashions."

"I have much to tell you," Letty replied as she sat on one of the armless farthingale chairs by the fireplace. She quietly awaited the questions she knew would be forthcoming. Her father leaned forward in his chair, and, after clearing his throat, began to speak.

"Letty, we have been distressed and concerned by the letters we have received from your aunt these past two months. Also the ones we received from you, for we felt you were not being entirely candid. This last letter we received from your aunt particularly concerned us," he said, holding up several closely written sheets. "If Henrietta had not said you were coming back, I should have gone to London to get to the bottom of the affair. We have heard what your aunt had to say, now we should like to hear your accounting. Tell us, please, what led to a duel being fought over you."

Letty clasped her hands in her lap and quietly and factually told the story of her attachment to Lord Courtney, her aunt's refusal to allow her to see him, and her pressure on Letty to accept the suit of Lord Satre, all culminating in her decision to elope with Lord Courtney, and her rescue by Lord Wakeford.

At the end of her recital there was silence in the parlor as her parents thought over what she had told them. Letty heard the ticking of the long-case clock in the corner and imagined that the beating of her heart was beginning to sound as loud through the room as she waited for a pronouncement from her father. At last he spoke.

"Although your aunt and cousin were not without blame in this affair, I am afraid that your behavior was not at all what it should have been. Your aunt was right to forbid you to see Lord Courtney, as subsequent events have borne out, and you should have obeyed her. We told you before you left that your aunt would stand in our place and that you owed her the obedience you would give us while you were a guest in her house. You do see that?"

"Yes," said Letty, looking ashamed. "But Lord

Courtney was the only person who was kind to me, or at least the only gentleman," she amended, thinking of Lady Wakeford. She went on to tell her parents of her social errors and the nickname she had been given, things she had left out of her letters home for fear of distressing her parents. "Then Aunt Henrietta pressed me so to accept Lord Satre's suit, and I could *not* like him. He made me feel uncomfortable, and he was quite as old as you, or even older, Papa."

Squire Biddle smiled slightly before replying. "Your aunt did not do well to press you to accept Lord Satre's suit against your will. However, you must realize she was concerned about your preference for Lord Courtney, and probably felt she was acting for the best. She wrote that Lord Satre is very wealthy, and that she could be sure his interest in you was not motivated by your fortune. You should have realized that no betrothal could be officially entered into without my approval, and that I would never force you to marry a person you could not care for."

"I know that now, Papa," Letty said. "But when I was in London, you seemed so far away." Her voice broke, remembering. Now that she was home, the fears she had had in London seemed foolish, but when she was in town, her home and family and its influence had seemed so very distant.

"I am sorry if I have failed you," she said contritely. "Please forgive me."

"Of course we forgive you, and you did not fail us. But I think you should write to Lady Hardwick and apologize for not obeying her as you should have and as she had the right to expect that you would. That, at least, you could do with honesty?"

"Yes, Papa," Letty agreed, if halfheartedly. It was true she had owed obedience to her aunt, but she did not think that all of Lady Hardwick's behavior to her had been motivated by concern for her welfare.

Noting her hesitation, her mother entered the conversation. "You must remember that you went to London at your own request, Letty. We do not say that your aunt was blameless in the affair. She was not. But perhaps there would have been less friction between you if you had been more obedient."

"Yes, Mama, I see that," Letty agreed.

The dressing-down at an end, the conversation turned to tales of Letty's happier experiences in London, and they talked together animatedly until it was time for dinner.

Letty found herself looking at the country with new eyes after her return to Derbyshire. The days no longer seemed dull, the entertainments no longer flat. She was even glad to see Thomas Goodman and his sisters again. His frank admiration was balm to her spirits. She did not miss London at all, except her friendship with Lady Wakeford.

She kept up a regular correspondence, which helped mitigate that loss. Lady Wakeford's letters were unsatisfying in one aspect, however, for she mentioned little about her brother. Letty wondered how Lord Wakeford was and what he was doing. Had he perchance found another girl to tease and occupy his mind now that his amusing "Letty

177

Loppet" was no longer in town?

Late that July, Letty received a letter in which Lady Wakeford described her first meeting with the new Lady Lockwood.

"She wore an elaborate robe of multicolored vertically striped satin worn over a full decorative petticoat of horizontally striped silk, topped with a triple-caped collar of figured silk. She was dripping with jewels, and no less than four ostrich plumes were displayed in her hair. The whole did not become her nearly so well as the gowns she used to wear. She was mightily pleased with the appearance she made, however, and unbent so far as to speak with me. It was most condescending of her, since as a married woman and countess she must take precedence over the unmarried daughter of a marquess. Indeed, she generously offered to assist me to make a match before I was quite at my last prayers. I thanked her and said that at the advanced age of one and twenty I had already reached them, but that she might use her offices to help Miss Alcock.

"The latest *on-dit* is that the new Lady Lockwood now considers her own mother to be beneath her consequence, and is rarely seen in her company."

Letty finished the letter and refolded the sheets, placing them in her escritoire. So, Sophie had achieved her goal of becoming a titled lady. Despite Sophie's deceit and unkind treatment of her, Letty wished her happiness. She could not deny, however, that she felt Lady Hardwick's failure to enter the higher realms of Society through her daughter was no more than she deserved.

The letter had made Letty feel rather lonely, and she decided to go for a ride. One of the best things about being back in Derbyshire was being able to ride her gentle mare, Acorn, again. She dressed in one of her new riding habits, of red-trimmed fawn, and started down the road to the village. To her surprise, she encountered Thomas Goodman walking up the road. He was usually busy working in the fields all day in the summer. The Goodmans' farm was very large and demanded the full attention of both father and son throughout the summer months.

"Good morning, Mr. Goodman," she called cheerfully.

"Good morning, Miss Biddle," he replied, stopping as she came abreast of him. "Is the squire at home?"

"No, he went to Lord Woodburn's this morning. He should be back this afternoon. Is it anything urgent?"

"No, I just wanted to ask his advice on a hunter Sir Archer has offered to sell my father. I can ask him another time."

"Help me down and I shall walk with you," Letty offered. Tom held her mount and gave her a hand as she slipped down from the sidesaddle. They walked slowly down the road together, Tom leading Acorn.

"I was glad to find you unchanged when you returned," Tom confided, his brown eyes observing her frankly. "I was afraid that after a Season in London you might return to Derbyshire a fine lady. Not that you aren't, I mean . . ." he added, and floundered as he searched for the right words.

"I know what you thought, Mr. Goodman," Letty said, laughing at his confusion. "At first there was a danger of that, but I found London was not at all as I expected it would be."

Tom looked at her questioningly, and Letty soon found herself confiding to Tom all that had happened to her in London. By mutual consent they turned off the main road and walked into the woods, where they sat together beneath an oak while Letty continued her story. She told him things she had told no one else but her parents, although she left out all about the duel and Lord Wakeford.

"And so it turned out they all despised the squire's daughter, although they respected her money, even if it was tainted by trade," she finished, a bitter note in her voice.

Hearing it, Tom reached for her hand and took it in his. "Those fine town gentlemen don't know real quality when they see it," he said indignantly. "You were wise to come home, where people accept you and value you for what you are. *I* liked you before you had any money, as did everyone else in the district."

Letty looked at Tom's honest face, now sober with concern, and smiled warmly. "Yes, you did," she said, overcome with a rush of affection and gratitude.

Her smile moved Tom to boldness. "Miss Biddle," he said suddenly and unexpectedly, "would you consent to become my wife? I have always admired you and wished to marry you, since we were children."

Letty, surprised by the unexpected declaration, said nothing for a moment, but continued to gaze into his eyes. She looked into his honest face, bronzed from the sun with all his days working in the fields, and felt a flood of warmth, love, and appreciation for his genuine goodness.

"I have taken you unawares," he said. "You will need time to consider."

A picture of a man with paler skin, chestnut hair, and amused green eyes flickered through Letty's mind, but she banished it ruthlessly. She had had no word from him; he had not even asked to be remembered to her in the letters she received from his sister. No doubt he had completely forgotten the girl he had labeled "Letty Loppet" and from whom he had derived so much amusement.

"No, I do not need time to consider," she answered. "I should be honored to be your wife, Mr. Goodman."

"Tom," he corrected her, his face lighting with joy. He looked at her as though he could not believe his good fortune, and then drew her into his strong arms. "I shall speak to your father in the morning," he said, and, turning her face to his, softly kissed her lips.

Letty felt very secure and safe in Tom's arms. His kiss was very unlike Lord Satre's disgusting assault on her lips, and it did not cause the tingling down her spine that the one she had received from Lord Courtney had, but it was warm and comforting, and that was what Letty wanted. She needed reassurance and protection. She had learned her lessons in London well, and would not pine again for life among the *haut ton*. Life as a farmer's wife would be much more appropriate for "Letty Loppet."

That same morning in London Lady Wakeford

was endeavoring to make out invitations to a musicale her mother planned for the next week, but was finding it difficult to concentrate on her task because of a rhythmic tapping noise coming from the other side of the room.

"Jules, do leave off playing with your whip and come sit down if you do not intend to ride."

"Sorry Emily, I have been feeling restless this morning," Lord Wakeford apologized, turning from the window where he had been standing, looking out and tapping his boots with his whip.

"You have been restless all summer," Lady Wakeford declared, lipping her pen into the inkwell and turning to face her brother.

"Yes, I suppose I have. It is quite dull in town with the Beau, Palmer, Prinny, and all the rest off in Brighton."

"Why do you not join them?"

"It does not appeal to me somehow," Jules confessed. "I must be getting on in years."

"Fustian. You are no older than Palmer, or the Beau, for that matter." Lady Wakeford looked at her brother curiously. It seemed to her that her brother's ennui dated from before the end of the Season and the departure of his friends for Brighton. To when Miss Biddle had left town, to be precise. She wondered if the two cared for each other more than they realized. She remembered Miss Biddle's concern for Jules the night of the duel. Miss Biddle never asked about Jules in her letters, but that could as easily denote interest as a lack of it.

"Miss Biddle has been most pressing in her invitation to me to stay with her family in Derbyshire," she said aloud. "If Mama agrees, I think I shall go

182

in September. Aunt Maud is planning to come to stay here with Mama and remain until Christmas, so she will not miss me. Do you not have a friend in Derbyshire who has asked you to partake of the hunting? Perhaps you could escort me," she suggested, watching his reaction to her words closely.

He appeared to be taken by the idea, for he left his position by the window and his face brightened.

"Yes, Lord Woodburn," he replied. "He has been asking me up for several years. That is an excellent idea. I shall be pleased to escort you to Derbyshire this autumn," he declared.

Chapter Twelve

Squire Biddle gave his consent to his daughter's betrothal to Thomas Goodman with some misgivings. He had nothing against Tom Goodman, he was a steady man and a hard worker, and would be a good and faithful husband. Nor did he think a squire's daughter above a farmer's son, or hesitate because of Letty's fortune. The Goodmans owned their own land, and were one of the most prosperous families in the district, not barring those of noble blood. What gave him pause was Letty's attitude. Although she claimed to love Tom, Squire Biddle rather thought his daughter did not know what love between a man and woman was. Well, perhaps Thomas Goodman would awaken her. He gave his blessing, but urged a long engagement.

Letty saw little of her betrothed during the rest of the summer, for he was busy with his father doing farm work. She did call on his mother occasionally, and endured the teasing of Tom's younger sisters good-naturedly. It had already been decided that she and Tom would live in their own house. Farmer Goodman owned a considerable amount of land, and his wedding present to his son would be a beautiful piece halfway between the Goodman farm and the squire's, where their house would be built.

On the whole, Letty was content with her betrothal, although there were times she would remember dancing through an elaborately decorated ballroom in the arms of Lord Arlington, Lord Courtney, or, most often, Lord Wakeford.

Her correspondence with Lady Wakeford flourished, but for a reason she did not understand herself she had not told Lady Wakeford of her betrothal to Thomas Goodman. Every time she received a letter from Lady Wakeford her omission made her feel guilty, but she quieted her conscience with the rationalization that it would be better to tell her in person, since Lady Wakeford planned to come stay with the Biddles in September.

As the summer was slowly transformed into fall, the social season of the country commenced. To the surprise of the inhabitants of the quiet Derbyshire district, this autumn promised to be a very full one, for several gentlemen who had had standing invitations to hunt chose this year to accept. No one connected this with the presence of the young heiress in their midst, but it was indeed she who was the attraction. The London beaus were not about to allow Miss Biddle's fifty thousand pounds to escape so easily. The scandal of the duel had long ago been replaced by newer *on-dits*. Besides, of what concern was a duel when the duns were at one's door? It took only a few discreet questions to find where Miss Biddle lived, and the prospective suitors remembered invitations issued long ago to hunt the Derbyshire countryside. If the squire and Mrs. Biddle suspected the truth, they did not share their suspicions with Letty, for they knew it would only make her uncomfortable. She seemed unaffected at hearing of the presence of the London gentlemen in the neighborhood, never suspecting she was the magnet that drew them there.

The only guest from London that Letty became excited about was Lady Wakeford. True to her promise, her friend wrote that she would be arriving the last week of September, and that her brother, who would be staying at Lord Woodburn's, would escort her there. This last news was a shock to Letty, and strangely unwelcome. She felt renewed guilt that she had not told Lady Wakeford of her betrothal, and wondered if the knowledge would have made a difference in Lord Wakeford's decision to come to Derbyshire. Then she scolded herself severely for making the assumption that knowing of her betrothal could make any difference in Lord Wakeford's plans. How could she be that full of conceit? Still, she dreaded their initial meeting.

As it turned out, Letty was spared meeting Lord Wakeford when Lady Wakeford arrived, for they came while she was out. Letty returned home one afternoon from a call on the Goodmans to find her friend talking easily with her mother. Lady Wakeford stood at her entrance, and, hesitating only a moment, they went to each other and embraced. Mrs. Biddle left the two friends alone, and they talked vivaciously for several minutes. Then, remembering the news she had not previously told Lady Wakeford, Letty informed her friend of her betrothal.

"You are engaged?" Lady Wakeford repeated with surprise. "Is this a recent thing? You did not mention it in your letters."

"No—" Letty hesitated. "I—I suppose I felt I would like to give you such information in person."

Lady Wakeford thought this rather strange, as an

engagement was normally something one wished to inform one's friends of immediately. "May I ask who he is?"

"He is Thomas Goodman, the son of a farmer in the district. They are one of the most prosperous families in Derbyshire," she added a little defensively, and then felt guilty for having felt the need to defend the Goodmans to Lady Wakeford. But she did not wish her London friend to think of them slightingly.

"I shall look forward to making Mr. Goodman's acquaintance," Lady Wakeford said, thinking that she would indeed be curious to meet this mysterious betrothed. Letty did not speak of him like a woman in love.

Lady Wakeford's wish was granted shortly, for the Biddles had been invited to supper at the Goodmans' the next evening, and the invitation was extended to include the Biddles' guest as well.

Letty had some misgivings as to whether Lady Wakeford would be able to fit in and be comfortable with the Goodmans. She remembered the exclusive behavior of many of the *ton* in London, but she had reckoned without the impeccable breeding of Lady Wakeford, whose perfection of manners allowed her to fit in anywhere. Lady Wakeford did not exhibit a trace of condescension in her manner toward the Goodmans. She greeted Mr. and Mrs. Goodman cordially, and admired their house and land with a sincerity that was not to be doubted.

Then the moment Letty had been anticipating most anxiously was upon her, and she presented Tom to Lady Wakeford. She need not have worried about that either. The two looked at each other frankly and

187

assessingly, and the smiles that came over the faces of both seemed to indicate that each approved the other.

After a hearty supper of partridge, hares, asparagus, and preserved gooseberries, Mrs. Goodman and the other women went in to the Goodmans' small, cozy parlor to talk while the gentlemen remained at the table to visit.

To the dismay of Mrs. Goodman, Tom's sisters, particularly young Betsey, monopolized Lady Wakeford's company, admiring her clothes and asking interminable questions about the latest London fashions and gossip. Only the arrival of the gentlemen put an end to their importunings.

Tom shooed his sisters away from Lady Wakeford, and Mrs. Goodman asked Letty if she would favor the company with a selection on the small square pianoforte that was the pride of the Goodmans' parlor. Letty complied good-naturedly, although she was not an accomplished performer. As she played several simple country airs, she was pleased to see that Tom and Lady Wakeford were conversing together. She had not needed to worry that her London friend would snub the Goodmans.

When Letty finished her meager repertoire, Mrs. Goodman asked Lady Wakeford to play, and she took Letty's place at the piano. Lady Wakeford's playing put hers to shame, Letty thought unenviously. The whole company was impressed with her skill. Entranced, Tom went to stand next to the piano so he could better admire her playing.

The Goodman sisters displayed their talent after Lady Wakeford finished, and then card tables were set up and the evening ended in a spirited game of whist.

The next morning the meeting Letty had been long dreading occurred. Lord Wakeford came to call, paying his respects to Squire and Mrs. Biddle, and thanking Letty for her invitation to his sister. His manner was polite but cold, and Letty wondered if she had imagined the times in London he had seemed so kind. This was more like the supercilious gentleman who had named her "Letty Loppet." He brought an invitation from Lord Woodburn to the Biddles for a ball to be held at Lord Woodburn's two days hence.

Letty dressed with great care for the ball at the Woodburns'. She told herself it was for the benefit of Tom, who would also be in attendance. Things were more democratic in the country, and prosperous commoners were regularly included in invitations to entertainments. In addition, Tom's three sisters were needed for dance partners. Letty chose one of her favorite gowns, one she had ordered in London but never before worn, a tunic dress of white edged in gold trim and worn over an underdress of deep blue silk. She threaded a white riband through her dark curls, and Daisy tied a silk flower in them. Letty completed her toilette with jeweled white-satin slippers, a painted chicken-skin fan, and a blue satin reticule. The image that smiled at her in the glass was quite satisfying, and she went downstairs to join the others with confidence.

Mrs. Biddle was clad in a diamond-figured buff silk gown with a lace flounce, and looked quite handsome. Lady Wakeford wore a simple chemise dress of white muslin with a gathered neckline, trimmed in green ribands. Her chestnut hair had been brushed until it shone, and she wore it in an unfashionable braid wound about her head that gave her an almost regal appearance. Squire Biddle, whose single concession to fashion was his waistcoat of white cotton dimity striped with pink and yellow silk embroidery, complimented the women, and the party set off for the ball in high good humor.

Lord Woodburn's estate was the largest in the district, and he had invited everyone in the area plus their guests. Letty was surprised at the number of London gentlemen present. She had known several had arrived in the district for hunting, but she was surprised to find that she knew most of them; in fact, most were former suitors. They made themselves known to her and requested dances, behaving as though the scandal of the duel and all in London had never happened. She allowed each only one dance, much preferring to dance with Tom and her Derbyshire neighbors. It irritated her that the London gentlemen seemed to be pursuing her even when they must have heard of her betrothal to Mr. Goodman. She did not realize that the London beaus did not take her betrothal seriously, thinking that of course she would prefer a gentleman like themselves to a hearty rustic like Mr. Goodman if she were given the chance.

Letty was standing next to her mother, catching her breath after the exertion of a long country dance, when, to her horror, she saw none other than Lord Satre advancing across the floor. She had not heard he was in Derbyshire. As he came up to her, all her old fears rushed back, but then, as she presented her mother to him, they just as abruptly receded. Mrs. Biddle, remembering her daughter's stories, was polite, but every inch an earl's granddaughter. Suddenly Letty felt foolish. Lord Satre could not hurt her here in Derbyshire among her friends and family.

"May I congratulate you on your betrothal and wish you every happiness?" Lord Satre was saying.

"Thank you, Lord Satre," Letty replied with dignity.

"I trust your betrothed would not object to your allowing me the pleasure of one dance?"

Letty politely accepted, and Lord Satre led her onto the floor. His words were impeccably civil, but Letty felt, from something she occasionally glimpsed in his eyes, that she had had a near escape in London.

To her relief, Lord Satre did not bespeak a second dance later in the evening. She saw him lead Lady Wakeford out next, and, to her surprise, saw him dance twice with Betsey Goodman. Letty wished she might avoid seeing him again, but he had told her he was a guest of Sir Archer's, so she supposed he would be included in all the neighborhood entertainments to come.

After her second dance with Tom, Letty was standing with her mother when Lord Wakeford approached and requested a dance with her. Letty felt an involuntary thrill at his appearance. He was dressed in the style the Beau was making *de rigueur*—blue coat, white waistcoat, tight-fitting dark blue pantaloons over striped silk stockings, black shoes with buckles, and a beautifully tied white cravat. She despised herself for the comparison she could not help but make to Tom, who looked neat but unfashionable in his suit of brown wool broadcloth.

Letty was disappointed in her dance with Lord Wakeford, however, for he seemed very cool and remote, causing her, in return, to be silent and withdrawn. Yet for all their coldness, they were very

191

much absorbed in each other. They danced past Tom and Lady Wakeford, who were partnered, and while they were observed closely by both, they did not notice either. When the dance ended, Lord Wakeford returned Letty to Mrs. Biddle and did not ask her to save another dance for him later that evening. Letty danced a third time with Tom, and she felt that she had indeed made the correct decision to accept Tom's offer. How she could have thought fondly of that cold London gentleman, she did not know.

With mixed feelings Jules watched Letty dance with her betrothed. Fool that he was, he had not understood the extent of his feelings for Miss Biddle until he had heard of her engagement to Mr. Goodman from Lord Woodburn. The news had been a shock. He had known then, he would have realized what he had been seeking since the end of the Season last summer, or why the usual pursuits of a London gentleman had suddenly seemed meaningless and paltry. He could not blame Letty for not being aware of his feelings. How could she have had the slightest inkling when he did not know himself and when he had been mainly responsible for making her a figure of fun to London Society? What was even worse, he could not even despise his rival, for Thomas Goodman's innate worth was evident for all to see.

Lord Wakeford had known that dancing with Miss Biddle would be torment, yet he had been unable to refrain from asking her. She was so beautiful, with her fair skin, dark curls, and deep blue eyes, and here in Derbyshire she had a self-assurance that had been lacking in London. If he had known she was engaged, he thought, he would never have come to Derbyshire. Now that he was here, he could not leave so soon, or he would insult his hosts, Lord and Lady Woodburn. He was so absorbed in his depressing thoughts that he did not hear his sister approach.

"A penny for your thoughts," Lady Wakeford said, and he started, surprised to find her standing next to him.

"Excuse me, Emily, my thoughts were elsewhere."

"Not very happy ones, from that scowl on your face. You had best erase it, or else Lord Woodburn will think his entertainment not to your liking."

Jules smiled ruefully and made an effort to erase the frown.

"Why did you not tell me Miss Biddle was betrothed before we came to Derbyshire?" he asked abruptly.

"I did not know of the betrothal," Emily said, fanning herself lightly. "It is quite odd. She has been betrothed to Mr. Goodman since July, yet not once did she mention it in her correspondence."

"That *is* odd," Jules replied thoughtfully. "Do you suppose it was because he is a farmer and she was ashamed to tell you?"

"No. After her experiences with some of the London *ton,* she may have hesitated to impart the news she was marrying a farmer, but I do not think that was the primary reason for her silence. It did quite puzzle me at first, but now I think I have figured it out."

"What was the reason, then?"

"I think Letty does not love Mr. Goodman."

"Not love Mr. Goodman?" Jules repeated. "Then why would she enter into an engagement with him?"

"Because she does not know she is not in love with him."

Jules looked at his sister in exasperation. "Don't be

enigmatic, Emily. Explain what you mean."

"Remember how unhappy Miss Biddle was in London. Society taunted her for her social blunders and made it clear that she was being accepted only because of her wealth. When she returned here to Derbyshire, Mr. Goodman's solid worth and sincere regard for her must have been balm to her bruised self-esteem. I think she accepted his offer out of gratitude for his genuine love and admiration, and mistook it for love."

Jules was uncomfortably aware that his words had been responsible for giving Miss Biddle some of her most unhappy times in London, but his sister's words gave him a flash of hope nevertheless. Then, just as suddenly, the hope vanished.

"Whatever her reasons for entering into the betrothal," he said, "it has been done. One must allow that Mr. Goodman is a worthy man."

"Too fine and worthy a man to be married out of gratitude," Lady Wakeford said. "I only hope that Miss Biddle and Mr. Goodman come to a realization of their situation before it is too late."

"I agree, but it is none of our affair," Jules said.

"I am not so sure of that," she replied so softly that Jules was not sure he heard his sister aright. Their host came to claim Lady Wakeford for a dance, and Jules was not able to pursue the conversation further, but her remarks made him regard her thoughtfully the rest of the evening. Could Emily be correct in her surmise about Miss Biddle's feelings? And why was his sister so concerned over the matter? It was not as though the object of Miss Biddle's affections was a bounder, as in the case of Lord Courtney. Was there another reason for her interest? He looked speculatively at Thomas Goodman, and then shook his head in derision at his momentary suspicion.

The morning after the dance at Lord Woodburn's, Tom came to the squire's and asked Letty to join him for a short walk. Surprised, for he was extremely busy with the harvest, Letty agreed.

Tom seemed to have something on his mind, for he walked slowly, gazing at the ground, a solemn expression on his face. When they were some distance from the house, he stopped beside a Spanish chestnut and addressed her.

"Letty, if you wish it, I am offering to release you from our engagement."

Letty looked at him in astonishment. "Why would you think I wished to be released?"

"There are so many fine gentlemen from London come to pay you court this autumn. I remember that you told me they want you only for your fortune, but I think even you must admit they are not all like that."

Lord Wakeford's face flashed through Letty's mind at his words, causing her to feel guilty.

"No—how can you suspect me of such inconstancy," she protested, looking into Tom's eyes. "Perhaps they are not all here in hopes of gaining control over my fortune, but none of them are equal to you in my eyes."

Tom looked at Letty searchingly, his brown eyes seeming to search her heart for the truth. Letty withstood his scrutiny, hoping her doubts did not show.

"If those are truly your feelings," he said at last, "but if you are not sure, Letty, if you are not *very* sure, it is better to say so now. Marriage is a very seri-

195

ous step, and a final one. It would not do for us to enter upon it if you harbor any doubts at all."

His words made Letty feel very small and unworthy. If she was honest with herself, thoughts of Lord Wakeford, the man who had been the cause of much of her distress in London, did often take the place of thoughts of Tom, the man who offered her his love and care. She was uncomfortably ashamed of herself. She looked up at Tom again, to find him regarding her steadily.

"I am sure that I do not wish to be released from the betrothal."

Tom ceased to demur, and reached for Letty and kissed her lips. As before, Letty felt a sense of warmth and safety at the touch of his firm lips upon hers. She responded shyly to his kiss, and then placed her head against his shoulder. Tom placed an arm around her back and regarded her quizzically.

"You are still a child, for all your Season in London," he said softly.

Letty was going to ask for an explanation of his words, but he started walking slowly back toward her home, and she walked silently beside him.

October came, and the days shortened. The gentlemen were all involved in hunting, but it was an activity they frowned on women sharing. Letty and Lady Wakeford spent many pleasurable hours together riding and walking.

One morning in mid-October, Lady Wakeford went to call upon Lady Woodburn. Letty, desiring some time by herself to think some things through, declined to go with her and went instead to ride by herself. Since Tom's unexpected offer to release her from their engagement, and his enigmatic last words that day, she had wondered if something in her behavior had given rise to Tom's doubts. She had to admit, when she was honest with herself, that when she saw Tom she did not feel the same as she did when she saw Lord Wakeford. She was always glad to see Tom, and she and Lady Wakeford often spent time at the Goodmans' home, but Tom's presence brought only a feeling of warmth and security. The sight of Lord Wakeford brought a feeling of insecurity and excitement — something like she had felt for Lord Courtney, she thought ruefully, before he had shown his true colors. Did that mean she loved Lord Wakeford and not Tom?

Her ride had brought her to the top of a rise, and, catching sight of the hunt, she stopped and dismounted under a Spanish chestnut to watch it go by. Fox hunting was a rough-and-ready sport, and the riders rode in a neck-or-nothing style, jumping hedges and hummocks. The best riders planned in advance how to keep up with the hounds, looking ahead and avoiding fields of heavy plow, cutting corners, and trying to avoid the paths other riders took.

A gust of wind blew Letty's red skirt and showered her with red and gold leaves. The movement seemed to catch the eye of one of the riders. He fell back from the others and rode toward her. As he drew near, she saw it was Lord Wakeford mounted on one of Lord Woodburn's bays. He waved and cantered up to her.

"I thought I recognized your little mare," he said, smiling. "It is much too fine a day to waste indoors, is it not?"

"Yes," Letty agreed. "I love the country in the autumn. It makes one feel so alive. The wind seems to demand one follow it, and the air is so clear and invigorating. How I do go on," she said in confusion and blushed.

Lord Wakeford smiled again and dismounted coming to stand with her beneath the tree.

"I know how you feel. I would like to have an estate in the country. My family does not have one, oddly enough. They have always been content to remain in London." He stopped speaking and joined her in appreciation of the scenery. They had a wide view of fields that appeared a patchwork of red, orange, yellow, and brown. A few white clouds hurried across the vividly blue sky.

Another gust of wind showered them with more leaves, and Lord Wakeford turned his attention to Letty, looking at her intently. Letty, knowing she must appear quite rosy and windblown, tried to look away, but his eyes locked with hers and a tension became palpable between them.

Suddenly he reached out and pulled her into his arms, placing his lips over hers. Letty, ashamed because this was what she knew she had been wanting, put up her hands to push him away, but instead found herself clutching at his coat and pulling him closer. His kisses became more and more demanding, and Letty responded avidly, powerful, strange feelings sweeping through her body. Abruptly Lord Wakeford lifted his head from hers and spoke huskily.

"Letty, you must cry off from your engagement. You love me, not Mr. Goodman."

His words brought Letty back to a sense of what she was doing and what her position was.

"I cannot love you," she cried in distress, pulling

198

away and turning from him, resting her hand on the trunk of the tree as she felt weak from his kiss.

"You do, Letty, admit it," he said from behind her, and placed his hands on her shoulders, turning her back to face him.

"I *must* marry Tom," she protested.

"No. You cannot marry one man when you love another. It would not be right."

"But I love him, too," Letty insisted.

"It is not the same love, and you know it. I have often observed you together the past weeks, and I know you do not feel for him as a woman should for the man she is to marry. Do you respond to his kisses the way you just responded to mine?"

Letty had no answer, knowing that what he said was true. They stood a moment in silence, Letty looking at the leaf-covered ground, Jules watching the play of emotions on her face.

"Think over what I have said carefully," he said after several minutes. "We shall discuss it again."

With that he remounted and went to find the hunt.

As Lord Wakeford rode away, Letty sank to the ground at the base of the tree, unmindful of her new London habit of velvet. The kiss had been a revelation to her. *That* was what she had known intuitively a kiss should be. Not disgusting like Lord Satre's, or warmly comforting like Tom Goodman's, or even only spine-tingling like Lord Courtney's. Lord Wakeford's kiss had contained the qualities of Lord Courtney's and Tom's, and added to them some powerful feeling that made her want to press closer and closer to Lord Wakeford and never let go.

Should she cry off from her engagement with Tom? He had offered to let her go, but she had refused. Could she hurt him now by asking to be released? As she contemplated her predicament, another thought occurred to her. If she did cry off from her engagement from Tom, what then? What were Lord Wakeford's feelings for her? He had not said he loved her, only that *she* loved *him*. Did he love her, or want her for his wife? Even if he did, what would happen when they went back to London? Would she be "Letty Loppet" to him again? Could he ever be truly happy with a simple squire's daughter from Derbyshire? She sat beneath the tree a long time, searching for the answers.

Chapter Thirteen

Letty spent an uncomfortable afternoon and evening after her encounter in the woods with Lord Wakeford. She was trying to decide whether she had done wrong by becoming engaged to Tom, or whether she simply had not known her own feelings. After a sleepless night, trying to arrive at a conclusion, something happened that put her own troubles from her mind. The Biddles and their guest were partaking of breakfast, when a servant came with a request that Squire Biddle speak with Mr. Goodman. A few minutes later the servant came back with a request that Letty join Mr. Goodman in the small parlor downstairs.

Wondering why Tom would wish to see her so early in the morning, Letty excused herself from the table and went downstairs. Tom was standing by the parlor window, apparently deep in thought. He turned at her step.

"What is it, Tom?" Letty asked in alarm, knowing from his expression that something must be terribly wrong.

"Betsey has left with Lord Satre."

"Lord Satre?" Letty replied. "Why?"

Tom's eyes expressed anguish.

"From the note she left, she believes that Lord Satre intends to marry her, but your father and I fear we have reason to suspect that is not his intention."

"Oh, dear," Letty cried, lowering herself into a chair. "How long ago did she leave? Do you think there is a possibility of overtaking them?"

"She has a two-hour start on us, but in actuality they have more of an advantage than that appears, for we have no idea where they could be going. That is why I wished to speak to you. You told me of Lord Satre's pursuit of you in London. Did he ever happen to mention an estate in this area?"

Letty's forehead creased in concentration as she tried to remember. "No, I cannot recall him ever mentioning one. Perhaps Lord Wakeford would know," she suggested. "I believe he is acquainted with Lord Satre."

"I suppose I shall have to take him into my confidence, although I had hoped to hide my sister's disgrace from as many as possible," he said heavily. "If you cannot help, the squire and I had best leave. Every minute we tarry lets them get that much farther ahead."

He went to Letty and dropped a brief kiss on her forehead.

"Godspeed, Tom," Letty said, pressing his hands in hers.

When Tom had left, Letty thought about the shocking occurrence. How was it none of them had ever noted the development of an understanding between Betsey and Lord Satre? Looking back, she supposed it *had* been there to see—she had often seen Lord Satre dancing and speaking with Betsey, but it had not seemed anything to cause alarm. Betsey was a giddy young girl and flirted with many of the gentlemen, and it had never occurred to Letty that Lord Satre could be seriously interested in a farmer's daughter. How naive she had been—a man might want a girl like Betsey for reasons other than marriage. She shuddered at the thought of young Betsey in Lord Satre's hands.

Reluctantly she stood up and went back upstairs to inform her mother and Lady Wakeford of the developments. Both were horrified by the news.

"I fear the situation is worse than Squire Biddle and Mr. Goodman imagine," Lady Wakeford informed her hosts gravely. "Lord Satre was a member of the notorious Hell-fire Club in his youth. I am glad they are going to ask Jules for his assistance. He may be able to help."

"The Hell-fire Club, what is that?" Mrs. Biddle asked.

"It is no longer in existence," Lady Wakeford explained. "It was active some years ago. Jules would not tell me much about it, but I do know its membership included many of the most unprincipled rakes of the time. Their motto was 'Do whatever you want to.' "

That is the man my aunt wished me to marry, Letty thought as Lady Wakeford spoke. Although, to be fair, it was possible Lady Hardwick had not been aware of the full extent of Lord Satre's disreputable past. A new thought struck her.

"It is my fault," she exclaimed.

Her mother turned to her in surprise. "Your fault? What do you mean?"

"If Lord Satre had not met me in London and decided to follow me here to continue to press his suit, he would never have met Betsey," she cried in dismay.

"That is in no way your fault," Lady Wakeford said. "You did not invite Lord Satre to Derbyshire, and had no way to keep him from coming had you known his intention."

"Perhaps," Letty acknowledged, "but I cannot help feeling partly responsible."

"You must not blame yourself," Mrs. Biddle seconded Lady Wakeford. "Do not distress yourself. Perhaps your father and Mr. Goodman will overtake them before any harm comes to Betsey."

Lord Wakeford had finished his breakfast and was preparing to go for a ride with Lord Woodburn, when a servant informed him that Squire Biddle and Mr. Goodman wished to speak to him on a matter of importance. His first thought was that something might be amiss with Letty, and he did not even stop to remove his banyan and put on a coat before hastening down to the salon.

"Squire Biddle, Mr. Goodman," he said as he entered the room. "I hope all your family is well?" he asked, looking at the squire.

"Yes, but I fear all is not well with Mr. Goodman's," the squire replied, and he and Tom proceeded to tell Lord Wakeford of Betsey's flight with Lord Satre.

Jules felt first a great sense of relief that the bad news did not concern the Biddles, and then was angry at himself, for Mr. Goodman's sister was in grave danger. He tried to think where they might have gone.

"Lord Satre does have a property near Loughborough," he said after a moment. "I believe they are most likely headed there, particularly if Satre's purpose is not honorable."

"I think there can be no doubt that his intention is

to ruin her," Tom said quietly. "A marquess would have no other use for a farmer's daughter."

As a member of the aristocracy, Jules felt a twinge of guilt at Tom Goodman's words. He knew many of his peers would have the view Tom had expressed.

"Then I think the best plan is for us to leave directly. Does your father go, too?" he asked Tom.

"No, he leaves the responsibility to me. His age will not permit him to undertake such a journey."

"Allow me one moment to prepare," Jules said. "It will take me no longer. We shall travel in my chaise; it will be swifter. Did either of you bring arms? It would be wise to take them. If you have not, I shall provide them."

The squire had thought to bring a pistol, but Tom was unarmed. Jules went quickly back to his chambers, where his valet helped him change, and then Jules sent him to order his chaise prepared. As his valet left the room, he took two pistols, and after a moment of thought put on his smallsword. Gentlemen rarely wore swords anymore, except to formal entertainments, but in dealing with a person like Satre, Jules felt he needed all the advantage he could get. He told Lord Woodburn a matter of urgent business required him to accompany Squire Biddle on a short journey, and that he was not sure when he would return.

Lord Woodburn, noting the sword, looked at his guest questioningly, silently asking if his help was needed, but Jules shook his head. He returned to the squire and Mr. Goodman, and as soon as they were informed the chaise was ready, left.

The three men rode in silence most of the journey, each immersed in his own thoughts. They stopped only to change horses and make inquiries of the workers to see if they had noticed an older gentleman traveling with a younger girl earlier that day. Jules's guess as to Satre's destination was evidently correct, for the two had indeed passed earlier. Slowly but surely the gap closed. At two in the afternoon, the ostler at a posting inn informed them that not only had he seen the people they were seeking, but that they were at that moment inside the inn.

Tom Goodman looked at Squire Biddle in surprise. "Why would they stop so early at an inn?"

"I suppose Satre felt that after Betsey's note was found, it would be assumed they had gone north to Gretna," Jules said. "Or that he would be so far ahead, it would make no difference." Silently Jules suspected the reason was probably far more sinister, but he did not voice his fears.

They ascertained what room Satre and Betsey were in, and deciding that surprise was their best weapon, went silently up the stairs and burst in, pistols in hand. The sight that met their eyes made Jules's finger tighten involuntarily on the trigger.

Betsey lay sobbing in a corner of the room, her dress torn and stained. Lord Satre was in his shirt-sleeves, sitting calmly at a table, a bottle of wine before him. At the sudden appearance of the men, his hand had gone to cover the butt of a pistol that lay on the table, but he surveyed them coolly. Betsey, on seeing her brother, ran to throw herself against his chest.

"Stay here while I summon the magistrate," Tom said to Jules, relinquishing his sister to the squire's care.

Lord Satre spoke, a sneering smile on his lips. "The girl came willingly. No magistrate would act in such a case."

"Then I demand satisfaction," Tom said angrily. "Name your seconds."

"Really," Lord Satre replied with a curl of his lip as he looked Tom up and down insolently. "This is turning into a farce of the poorest quality. I could not sully my honor by dueling with a farmer's son. One meets only one's peers on the field of honor."

Tom's face turned purple with rage, and he advanced toward Lord Satre, but the squire restrained him with a hand on his shoulder.

"You cannot say I am not your equal," Jules said quietly from his position by the door.

"This is not your fight," Tom said, turning to him.

"He is correct, it is none of your affair," Lord Satre echoed.

"Then I shall make it mine," Jules said, and, removing one of his gloves, he stepped forward and slapped Lord Satre across his face with stinging force.

Lord Satre's eyes narrowed at the insult. "As you wish. If it is satisfactory to you, we shall dispense with the services of seconds, since I doubt men of suitable rank are to be found here."

Jules agreed. "Let us remove to a suitable place."

"This is as good as any," Lord Satre replied, motioning about the room. "I see you wear a sword."

The squire and Tom looked at Jules questioningly, for it would be difficult to fight in the confined space of the room. However, Jules indicated his agreement and asked the squire and Tom to leave, telling them to keep the innkeeper from interfering should he hear the disturbance.

Tom hesitated, not liking to leave the punishment of Lord Satre to another man, but the reality was that he could not otherwise be revenged for his sister.

A farmer, even with the support of Squire Biddle, could not touch a man of the aristocracy. A duel was inevitable now, in any case, for Lord Satre could not allow Lord Wakeford to leave after the insult he had dealt him, so it was out of his hands. Reluctantly, he left the room to tend to his sister.

As he took off his coat and prepared for the duel, Jules realized that the confined fighting space was likely to lead to the duel being a deadly one, and he also realized that was probably Satre's intent. Undoubtedly he was a very skilled swordsman. Jules did not fear Satre would cheat, as had Courtney. Satre would have no need. As he faced Lord Satre, who was also ready for the duel to commence, Jules did not feel the fatalistic calm he had during his duel with Lord Courtney, but felt keenly alert.

Jules withdrew his smallsword, which had been a gift from his father, abstractly admiring the beauty of the silver hilt with its inset enamel medallions. Lord Satre's sword hilt was more elaborate, heavily decorated with paste jewels.

As the duel began, Jules put his left hand behind his back in the manner of the German style, feeling this would be more to his advantage in the confined space. As he had suspected, Lord Satre was very skilled and had a great sense of form and timing.

Jules found himself forced to retreat around the table, although he knew attack was the best strategy. He was managing to hold his own, until, to his dismay, he stepped backward against a chair, and in the split second his attention was diverted, Lord Satre lunged and cut his arm.

Jules managed to keep hold of his sword, but he knew he now must attack with deadly intent, for if he were to bleed too much, he would lose the strength in his arm. His perceptions incredibly heightened by his imminent danger, Jules saw by a momentary widening of the pupils in Satre's pale gray eyes that he was going to attack. He moved quickly aside and parried the lunge, at the same moment delivering a lightning riposte. He felt Lord Satre's sword graze his side, but Jules's blade went home, passing through Lord Satre's breast. Satre's hold on his sword slackened, and Jules easily disarmed his opponent.

"I shall call a surgeon to see to you," Jules said curtly.

Lord Satre shook his head. "My wound is not mortal. I believe a rib deflected your blade from a vital spot. I shall care for myself." He made an almost imperceptible bow.

Jules did not acknowledge the obeisance, and saw by Satre's expression that he understood that Jules did not consider Satre *his* peer.

With a final contemptuous look Jules left the room in search of his companions.

Jules observed the tenderness of Thomas Goodman toward his sister on their return journey with approbation. He would deliver them to their farm first and then go to the squire's to have his wound taken care of. In their haste to leave the inn, he had waited only to have it bound with clean cloths.

He thought wryly how he had gone through six-and-twenty years without fighting a single duel, and now since meeting Miss Biddle, he had been involved in two within the space of six months.

When they arrived at the squire's and walked into the stone-paved entrance hall, Mrs. Biddle, Letty, and Lady Wakeford appeared from the parlor. At the sight of the blood that had soaked through Jules's coat, Letty let out a cry and she and Lady Wakeford ran to his side. Jules made light of his wound, calming their fears.

"Mr. Goodman and Betsey?" Lady Wakeford asked, her eyes finishing the question.

"Mr. Goodman is unharmed and has taken his sister home, but I fear we were too late."

Mrs. Biddle observed the situation and quietly took charge, sending for the housekeeper and going to get the things necessary to dress Jules's wounds. She returned shortly and took him to a bedchamber, telling Letty and Lady Wakeford to stay away until she came for them.

Letty and Lady Wakeford waited in anxiety while Mrs. Biddle and the housekeeper dressed Jules's wounds and the squire sent a servant to fetch Jules's valet and inform Lord Woodburn that his guest would be staying at the squire's several days.

"I feel for the Goodmans," Lady Wakeford said to her friend. "How distressing it must be to have their daughter ruined. I like Betsey. She is flighty, but had no real badness in her."

Lady Wakeford's words made Letty realize with a start that she had not been thinking of the Goodmans at all, but only of Lord Wakeford, and felt ashamed.

Mrs. Biddle came to the door, her smile reassuring. "Lord Wakeford's wounds are not serious. His side was only grazed, and the cut on his arm is a clean one. I have given him a sleeping draft, so you will not be able to see him until the morning," she said, and returned to her patient.

Late that evening, Tom Goodman came to the door. He talked to Letty and Lady Wakeford, telling them his sister was with his mother and was as well as could be expected. "As soon as she is recovered, we plan to send her to live with my mother's sister and her husband in Lancashire, where people will not know of her disgrace. I feel sure they will take her in and provide her a home."

"It will be the best thing," Lady Wakeford agreed.

For a moment the three sat soberly and silently as they thought of the spirited young Betsey. What a high price she had paid for her foolish desire to marry into the aristocracy.

In the days that followed, Letty waited on Lord Wakeford when her mother allowed her to, feeling both beholden to him for his actions in Tom's behalf, and responsible for his willingness to involve himself, and the resulting wounds.

"You spoil me quite abominably," he said to her one morning when she brought him his breakfast on a tray. He was reclining on a sofa in the morning parlor, his pale skin almost white with the loss of blood.

Letty only smiled, and, placing the tray on the table, turned to leave, but he caught at her skirt and held her. When she turned around to protest, he smiled disarmingly and patted the sofa next to him, asking her to sit and visit a moment.

"I promised you a renewal of the conversation we had a certain day in the woods," he began.

"I must ask you not to reopen that conversation," Letty interrupted.

"Oh?" Lord Wakeford replied. "Are you going to tell me your feelings have changed? I shall not believe it. For your care of me during my convalescence here has shown me quite clearly they have not."

"No, my feelings have not changed," Letty admitted. "But do you not see that after what happened to

Betsey I cannot jilt Tom? I cannot be the cause of yet more unhappiness to his family."

"His sister's ruin had nothing to do with you."

"That is what my mother and your sister tell me, but I still feel partly to blame. Even if I did not, I could not make Tom unhappy by calling our betrothal off. He is too fine a man to be treated so."

"Did it ever occur to you that he is too fine a man for you to marry when you do not love him, and, in fact you love another?" Jules asked, unconsciously echoing his sister's words of four weeks earlier.

Letty turned away in distress, and started to rise, but Lord Wakeford grasped hold of her with unexpected strength and pulled her down to him. He began to kiss her and caught off guard, Letty responded to his insistent kiss. As soon as he felt her return his kiss, Lord Wakeford stopped and lay back on the sofa, a satisfied look on his face.

"Are you going to tell me you respond to Thomas Goodman like that?" he asked. "If you cannot tell me that you do, you should not be marrying one man when you long for the touch of another."

Letty jumped up and made for the door. Halfway across the room, she faced Lord Wakeford, an expression of distress and determination on her face.

"I must ask you not to importune me again, Lord Wakeford. Whether you consider it binding or not, I am betrothed to another man. Your action may have taken me unawares, to my shame, but I shall never again allow myself to be put in such a position," she declared, and left the room, her head held high.

Chapter Fourteen

Letty avoided Jules until he left the following morning, braving her parents' censure by not going down to take her leave of him as was proper. She stood by the window of her bedchamber, watching his sister give him a hug and the squire help him personally into the carriage. As the carriage drove off, taking Lord Wakeford back to Lord Woodburn's, Letty turned from the window, a feeling of depression settling on her. She did not feel up to talking to anyone or joining in any amusements, and told Daisy to inform her mother she had a headache.

The next day she forced herself to go downstairs and join the others, but she was still feeling miserable. She had no one to confide in, although she suspected both her parents and Lady Wakeford knew something was troubling her. She tried to shake off her depression of spirits, and forced herself to participate in the neighborhood entertainments the next week. She was quiet, but this was not noticed since everyone in the neighborhood was somewhat subdued in the wake of Betsey Goodman's disgrace. Lord Satre had sent a servant to collect his belongings from Sir Archer's, and did not return to the district.

Letty and Lady Wakeford often rode to the Goodmans', and Letty noticed how Mrs. Goodman seemed to lean on Lady Wakeford and ask her for advice. She felt guilty that she was not offering more support to Mrs. Goodman herself, but she was unable to because she was so immersed in her guilt and misery over the situation with Tom.

The next week brought November, and Letty still had not resolved her dilemma. She avoided both Lord Wakeford and Tom. Tom seemed not to mind, and the times he did see her did not push to set a date for their wedding, although he had more free time now that the harvest was in.

The day of the hunt ball arrived. It was to be Lady Wakeford's last entertainment, for she and her brother planned to return to London afterward.

That morning, Letty and Lady Wakeford went for a ride together, as was their custom when the weather allowed. Lady Wakeford seemed quite preoccupied, and did not answer several questions Letty put to her. They reached the top of a hill and halted, looking out over the countryside. The colorful leaves had fallen, leaving bare skeletons stark against the gray sky.

Abruptly, Lady Wakeford turned to Letty.

"Miss Biddle, would you forgive the presumption of a close friend asking a personal question?"

"Please feel free to ask me anything you wish," Letty replied politely, surprised at her request.

"Do you love Mr. Goodman?" Lady Wakeford asked, a delicate flush suffusing her face.

"Of course I do," Letty replied, surprised and somewhat embarrassed by the question.

"I mean *really* love him," Lady Wakeford pressed,

214

regarding Letty with a strangely intent look. "As you love my brother," she ended quietly.

Letty felt her cheeks redden, and she looked away in confusion. "I don't know what you mean."

"I think you do," Lady Wakeford contradicted her friend quietly.

"Lady Wakeford, I *must* love Tom," Letty said, turning back to face her friend. "He is always so good and kind, not like the fine gentlemen I met in London. I cannot repay that by jilting him."

Lady Wakeford was silent a moment, reaching forward to stroke her mount. She straightened and spoke again.

"I understand your scruples, and they do you credit. But is it fair to Mr. Goodman, feeling as you do for my brother?"

Letty said nothing, making no attempt to deny her affection for Lord Wakeford.

"Do you not think, Miss Biddle," Lady Wakeford persisted, "that Mr. Goodman deserves the kind of love from his wife that you have for Jules?"

"Of course he does, but —" Letty faltered, unable to answer.

"Has it occurred to you that Mr. Goodman might also have observed your affection for Jules and *wish* to be released?" Lady Wakeford pursued relentlessly.

"He did ask me once," Letty said slowly, "but I thought it was because of Lord Satre, and the others who came here from London this autumn."

Now Lady Wakeford looked away, tapping her boot with her crop. She seemed to come to a decision and turned resolutely to Letty. "Miss Biddle, would it make it an easier decision for you if I told you that *I* love Mr. Goodman?"

Letty looked at her friend in astonishment. She knew that Lady Wakeford liked the Goodmans, but in love with Tom? She would never have dreamed of it!

"You?" she burst out. "But you are a marquess's daughter."

Lady Wakeford looked at her wryly. "My rank does not prevent my caring for one not of the same rank."

"Does Tom return your feeling?" Letty asked bluntly. "And if he does, why has he not asked to be released?"

"Mr. Goodman is much too honorable to ask to be released from the engagement," Lady Wakeford said. "It must be the woman who does that. As for your other question, Mr. Goodman has never *told* me he returns my affections. Again, he is much too honorable. Yet I know that he does. Words are not necessary—I am sure you understand . . ." she trailed off.

Letty did understand. How often had a look, a gesture, conveyed so much more than words could between her and Jules. Another possible obstacle occurred to her.

"Your family would not approve if they knew you had conceived a *tendre* for a farmer."

"My family will not be overly pleased," Lady Wakeford admitted. "But they had begun to give up hope I would ever marry, and I think they could be persuaded. If they are not, it will make no difference."

Letty was aware of the difficulty Lady Wakeford had had in sharing her personal feelings with her.

"Thank you for confiding in me," Letty said, "I shall think about what you have said."

"That is all I ask," Lady Wakeford replied. She

smiled briefly and a little sadly at Letty, and, turning her mount, cantered back toward the Biddles'.

Letty followed slowly, thinking all that had happened was much too confusing and complicated. Halfway back she came to an abrupt decision and turned in the direction of the Goodmans' farm. She saw one of Tom's sisters, who directed Letty to the stables. Tom heard her riding up and emerged from the stable, a look of surprise on his face.

"Isn't my mother in the house?" he asked, assuming she had come to call on Mrs. Goodman.

"It is you I wish to speak with," Letty explained. "May I have a moment of your time?"

"Of course," Tom replied, and helped her dismount as a groom came to take her mare.

The two walked a distance from the farm, to the shores of a small lake, where they sat down. Letty looked at Tom soberly. It was difficult to gather the courage to speak, but she knew she must.

"Tom, I have come to see that the affection I have for you is not the kind of affection a woman should have for the man she marries. Although I have the greatest respect and love for you, I know now we should not suit."

"I wondered if you would come to see that," Tom agreed.

"You knew?" Letty said, surprised and a little miffed that he seemed not to be at all disappointed. Mentally she chastised herself. "Why did you not ask to be released?"

"I hoped you would come to see for yourself."

Letty smiled at him ruefully, and then laughed at her lack of perception. "I have been a slowtop, haven't I?" she asked. Tom grinned at her and put an

217

arm around her shoulders, hugging her to him with brotherly affection.

They sat in companionable silence a moment, Letty thinking of Lady Wakeford's revelations to her that morning. She decided to try to help her friend. Tom might not dare aspire as high as Lady Wakeford if she did not.

"I might not have come to see my true feelings had it not been for a hint from a friend," she essayed.

Tom's face was suddenly suffused with red. "I think I know the 'friend,' " he replied, looking conscious.

Letty hesitated to be more explicit. "My friend's happiness means a great deal to me," she said. "I hope it means as much to the one with the power to ensure it."

"It does," Tom responded briefly, but the look on his face told Letty he understood all she had left unspoken. She stood up and Tom followed suit. They walked back to the farm in total harmony.

Letty returned home feeling very alone. Not wanting to talk to Lady Wakeford, she went directly to her room and summoned Daisy to help her prepare for the hunt ball. The hunt ball was the social occasion of the year. It was held at Sir Archer's estate, since he had the largest ballroom.

Letty had saved one of the gowns she brought from London particularly for the hunt ball. It was a closed robe of dull red silk with brocaded flowers of gold, yellow, red, and green. The autumn colors flattered Letty's complexion, and she was pleased with her image in the glass. She added a lace collar to the dress, and Daisy arranged ribands and plumes in her dark curls. Letty's spirits began to lift, and she went to join the others with a smile on her lips.

Mr. and Mrs. Biddle were already dressed and waiting in the parlor. Mrs. Biddle was looking her most handsome in a gown of aubergine taffeta, and Mr. Goodman wore his usual suit of drab wool broadcloth, his brocaded waistcoat adding a touch of color.

Lady Wakeford came down soon after Letty, looking beautiful in a white muslin gown embroidered with green and gold garlands and bows. A gold fringe decorated the hem, and she wore a silk fichu whose ends attached to the green sash about her waist with a jeweled fichu buckle. Her thick chestnut hair was arranged in a cascade of curls, and a plume arched over her forehead. The party set out for the ball happy in the knowledge that they all looked their best.

When they arrived at the ball, Letty was claimed by Tom for the first dance, and she appreciated his thoughtfulness. She did not want people to be curious, as they would be if he had not danced first with her. He smiled at her affectionately, and Letty knew she still had her friend.

After his dance with Letty, Tom asked Lady Wakeford to partner him. As the fashionable Lady Wakeford danced with the farmer, the difference in their ranks seemed to melt away in the warmth of their mutual affection. Letty felt a pang of envy and turned away to see Lord Wakeford approaching. A medley of conflicting emotions gripped her, and her heart fluttered. He looked incredibly attractive, and she took in every detail of his appearance. He was wearing a ruffled linen shirt, a white linen cravat, a coat of olive green, drab kerseymere breeches, white-silk clocked stockings, and black-buckled shoes.

"May I have this dance, Miss Biddle?" he asked when he reached her side, the look in his eyes belying the formality of his words.

She curtsied in acceptance, and they danced together silently. Aware of her newly free status, Letty felt able to respond to his bold looks, and flirted daringly. When the dance ended, he did not relinquish her, but drew her out of the room and through the hall to a small parlor. He closed the door behind them and stood before it, folding his arms over his chest and looking at Letty sternly.

"This is quite enough of your nonsense. If you won't call off your betrothal, I *will.*"

Now was the time for Letty to tell Lord Wakeford that her engagement was at an end, but she hesitated. She knew she loved him, but she still did not know if he loved her. And what of her provincial manners and modest background?

"I meant what I said," Lord Wakeford proclaimed as Letty made no response. "In fact, I think I shall go to speak with Mr. Goodman now." He turned and placed his hand on the door, when Letty's voice stopped him.

"There is no need for you to speak to him. I have already broken off our betrothal."

"You did? When?" Lord Wakeford exclaimed, turning to look at her searchingly.

"This morning. Your sister persuaded me. It was quite a lowering experience," she continued. "I had the feeling Tom was relieved to be released."

"Then he deserves to lose you," he proclaimed, going to stand before Letty. "Why did you not tell me?"

Letty was silent and stared fixedly at the gilt claw feet of a chair next to her. Lord Wakeford took her chin in his hands and lifted her face to his. "Tell me," he commanded.

"I cannot," she said, breaking away.

"I shall force you to tell me. I am not going to lose you again. I have fought two duels because of you, followed you to Derbyshire, and been rivals with a bounder, a lecher, and a farmer for your hand. What more need I do to prove my love?"

At his last word Letty's eyes opened wide. "You love me?" she asked wonderingly. "You *love* me?"

"Of course I love you, dear goosecap," Jules said softly, and drew her into his arms, kissing her tenderly.

When she could speak, Letty voiced her last fears. "But what of when we return to London? Will I become 'Letty Loppet' to you again?"

Lord Wakeford looked steadily into Letty's eyes and softly caressed her face. "You will always be my 'Letty Loppet.' I would have you no other way," he said, willing her to understand that he loved her as she was.

"My provincial manners will not embarrass you?"

"Your manners will never embarrass me. In fact, I find I have become quite fond of all country things and plan to rusticate often. I even think to purchase an estate in Derbyshire."

"A splendid idea!" Letty beamed, believing in Lord Wakeford's love at last. "I predict your sister will be a frequent visitor until her farmer gets courage enough to come up to scratch."

"That is the way of it? I had suspected something of the sort. But enough of other lovers," he said, drawing her into his arms again. And Letty knew she belonged there forever.

THE ROMANCES OF LORDS AND LADIES
IN JANIS LADEN'S REGENCIES

BEWITCHING MINX (2532, $3.95)

From her first encounter with the Marquis of Penderleigh when he had mistaken her for a common trollop, Penelope had been incensed with the darkly handsome lord. Miss Penelope Larchmont was undoubtedly the most outspoken young lady Penderleigh had ever known, and the most tempting.

A NOBLE MISTRESS (2169, $3.95)

Moriah Landon had always been a singularly practical young lady. So when her father lost the family estate over a game of picquet, she paid the winner, the notorious Viscount Roane, a visit. And when he suggested the means of payment — that she become Roane's mistress — she agreed without a blink of her eyes.

SAPPHIRE TEMPTATION (3054, $3.95)

Lady Serena was commonly held to be an unusual young girl — outspoken when she should have been reticent, lively when she should have been demure. But there was one tradition she had not been allowed to break: a Wexley must marry a Gower. Richard Gower intended to teach his wife her duties — in every way.

SCOTTISH ROSE (2750, $3.95)

The Duke of Milburne returned to Milburne Hall trusting that the new governess, Miss Rose Beacham, had instilled the fear of God into his harum-scarum brood of siblings. But she romped with the children, refused to be cowed by his stern admonitions, and was so pretty that he had the devil of a time keeping his hands off her.